Finding Shelter

Steel Security #1

Charity Parkerson

Contents

Copyright

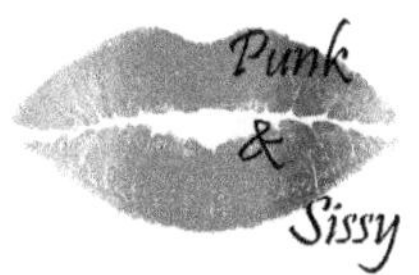

—Warning: This book is intended for readers over the age of 18. Some of my books contain allusions to past abuse and trauma.

Editor: BZ Hercules & Consultants

Cover art: Temptation Creations

Introduction

Nothing can top being assigned to protect his ex's dad. Unless he falls in love with him, of course.

Years ago, Kash thought he would spend the rest of his life with Valon. Then Valon got famous and everything changed. Nowadays, Kash walks a little on the wrong side of the law. The last thing Kash expects is to get offered a job protecting Valon's dad, Ledger. Even more surprising, Kash accepts. He needs a place to chill for a while anyway. Surely nothing could go wrong.

Ledger has always had mixed feelings about Kash. At one time, Ledger fully believed Kash would be his son-in-law one of these days. Then Valon's band skyrocketed to the top of the charts, and they were over. As Valon's father, it's his job to steer clear of Kash. Unfortunately, there's something about Kash. Face to face, he doesn't feel the loathing Valon likely expects. He feels something else when he sees Kash, something way worse.

Finding Shelter is the first book in Charity Parkerson's Steel Security series. These showcase some of the toughest bodyguards in the country as they fall hard for men they never see coming.

Chapter One

IT HAD TO BE a concert. That was all Kash could think as he pushed his way through the massive crowd. Kash's cousin, Steel, had offered Kash this gig. Steel owned a chain of security offices around the country, supplying bodyguards and various other security services to people in need. Since Steel was a cousin from his dad's side of the family, they really hadn't gotten to know each other before Kash went looking for any family he might have when he turned eighteen. But when Steel had called, saying he was short-handed and needed Kash's help, Kash accepted. Family helped family. Since Kash needed to get out of sight for a while anyhow, the opportunity had come at the perfect time. Kash couldn't claim Steel hadn't warned him ahead of time. Body-guard for a rockstar's dad hadn't sounded horrible, except for the part where said rockstar was Kash's ex. Still, Kash hadn't expected to see Valon this soon, if at all. Valon's band Backlash was currently on tour. Since they were in their hometown, it made sense for Valon's father, Ledger, to be here. At Valon's concert. Backstage. Fuck his life. He hoped with all his being that Ledger wanted to head out before the crowd dispersed and made traffic a nightmare. Preferably before Valon left the stage.

The venue's security escorted him through the mob of people toward where Ledger hid to watch the show. Kash's feet slowed as he neared the stage. He couldn't stop himself from pausing to stare. There he was. Valon had really done it. He was a star. Kash's throat swelled as he listened to the crowd singing along. Wow. Valon had to be on top of the world with thousands of people here just for him. Even though it had cost him everything, Kash had wanted this for him. He supposed they kind of hated each other now.

Valon's eyes slid his way. He stopped dead, going completely silent. The band stopped playing ten seconds behind him.

Confused chatter rolled through the building.

A bright smile lit Valon's face. "Holy shit. Is it really you?"

The crowd followed Valon's line of sight. All heads turned his way along with a spotlight. Goddamn it. So much for slipping quietly away from his old life.

Now wasn't the time to rage. A microphone was shoved in his face. Kash smiled and spoke through gritted teeth. "Yeah."

Valon moved to the edge of the stage and sat, forcing security to pool in one place and work double time to hold back the crowd.

Valon's gaze never wavered from Kash. He pointed at Kash while turning his attention to the crowd. "This was my best friend all through high school, Kash. Say hi, Kash." He focused on Kash again with an evil-looking smile stretching his lips.

Wanting to throttle Valon wasn't an unfamiliar feeling, but he hadn't missed it. "Hi."

Valon shook his head. "I'm blown away to see you here. How have you been?"

Kash had to pry his back teeth apart to answer. He saw the wicked glint in Valon's eyes. He enjoyed Kash's irritation. "Good. Looks as if you have been too." There, they could stop this, and Valon could get back to what everyone paid him to do.

Valon glanced around, speaking to the crowd again. "Did you guys know this is who convinced me to drop out of college and pursue my dreams?"

Whistles and cheers nearly stole Kash's hearing.

Valon stood. "That's why I'm stupid. Good seeing you." Valon burst into song, picking up right where he had left off as he danced away.

Kash shook his head and let security lead the way. Maybe Steel had known what he was doing after all. First reunion complete, saving Kash from drama. He supposed it could have gone worse. With any luck, he wouldn't have to talk to him again.

Kash had thought way too much about seeing Ledger again. He was almost shocked speechless as Ledger came into sight. The salt and pepper hair

Kash remembered was now solid white. His white beard was neatly trimmed. Ledger's shirt strained at the biceps, fighting for its life against Ledger's bulging muscles. While Ledger had always kept in shape, this was a whole new level.

Kash's surprise turned him dumb. "Why do you need me? Look at you." He spoke as loudly as he could to be heard while simultaneously hoping Ledger didn't hear.

Ledger turned at the statement. The first moment of surprise—hopefully—gave away his true feelings. Happiness lit his navy eyes before immediately turning baffled. "Hey!" He met Kash halfway, out of sight of the stage, and hugged Kash. The way he slapped Kash across the back felt exactly like a grown man trying to burp another grown man. Kash had all sorts of dumb thoughts, hoping to stop the huge, super-idiotic one from coming through—like how it felt a little too amazing in Ledger's arms. He might have had a few daddy issues in his life. Kash wasn't ashamed.

Ledger pulled away, but he didn't let go of Kash. He held Kash's shoulders and studied him. "Damn. You've changed."

Kash couldn't deny it. The last time Ledger saw him, Kash had thirty pounds less muscle and only two tattoos. Now that ink covered his entire torso and arms. "I've changed? Look at you."

Ledger took a step back. "Yeah, well." He cleared his throat. "Why are you back here? That sounded rude, but you know what I mean. Obviously, I heard Valon talking to you just now, but I thought maybe you were just here to see the show."

It was as if a smile had been permanently etched on his face. Kash made a dismissive gesture. "I get what you mean. I'm not easily offended, but I'm surprised Steel didn't give you a heads-up. He's assigned me to be your bodyguard." He had to yell every word to be heard. It was loud as hell backstage. Kash watched the horror and confusion grow in Ledger's expression as Kash's words sank in before an uncomfortable-looking smile took over. Kash couldn't take it. He rushed to fix things. "If you're not okay with me, you absolutely can ask for someone else. I'll call Steel and tell him to make the switch. Hell, I don't even know why I was sent here. It looks like you can handle yourself."

The discomfort vanished. Ledger became the man Kash remembered. "No. You caught me off guard, but this is actually perfect. I fought pretty hard against Valon on the whole bodyguard thing. I mean, I'm just some old man. But I know you, and that makes things a lot more comfortable for me. It'll just be like it used to be with you always under my roof."

Ledger did not sound comfortable, nor had it been comfortable under Ledger's roof. At least not toward the end there, but Ledger looked determined. Kash didn't know what to do next, but calling Steel made the most sense. Ledger had always gone above and beyond for him. Kash wouldn't put him in this position. Not again.

Goddamn. That was all Ledger could think. Kash looked amazing and bitter as hell. Damn. Ledger had truly hoped Kash disappearing into the world meant he was somewhere healed from all this. Considering everything about Kash screamed angry bad boy, it didn't seem as if time had changed anything. Surely Valon had to know Steel Security planned to send Kash. Maybe he had even arranged for that, considering how angry Ledger had been over the guard thing. No matter how many angles he looked at things, he couldn't imagine this being a good idea.

He motioned for Kash to come sit with him in the chairs set up on the side stage, where they could watch out of sight from the crowd. Ledger shouted over his shoulder as he went. "Come on. The show is almost over." What would happen then? He had been told his bodyguard would live with him. At least until some shit died down. The plan was that new guards would come in on rotation to give his personal guard a break, but Steel hadn't said shit about that full-time guard being his son's ex. Of course, it was very likely Steel hadn't known they knew each other. Either way, Ledger needed the excuse of watching the concert to take a moment to process.

Kash had offered to get someone else. The suggestion had immediately punched Ledger in the chest. Then Kash had nervously rambled, certain Ledger wanted nothing to do with him, and he couldn't let Kash walk away thinking Ledger hated him. He didn't. While it was Ledger's job to always take Valon's side, this was one place where utter confusion existed alongside so much gray area he couldn't see.

Damn, he took up a lot of space now. Ledger supposed the same could be said of him, but wow. Ledger couldn't stop looking at Kash from the corner of his eye. His hands were tattooed. His everything was covered in ink. There were scars on his knuckles that hadn't been there before. What the fuck had happened to him in the last five years?

Ledger wanted to ask, but it was too loud and not the time. He forced his eyes toward the stage and watched his son own the world. Ledger couldn't be prouder of him. Without thinking, he rubbed his chest. There was an empty hole where his son used to be. Nowadays, he looked like the star he was—hair dyed silver and brushing his shoulders. Valon's face showed every cut line from never eating and always being on the move. Ledger blew out a slow breath. He didn't know Valon anymore. That hurt way more than anyone could understand. It had just been them since his ex-husband abandoned them the moment Valon had turned eighteen. They had thrown a huge birthday bash that lasted for hours. When it was over, Ry had grabbed two packed suitcases Ledger hadn't known about and walked out the door. Ledger wanted to say he hadn't seen it coming. Unfortunately, a few months before he left, Ry had started talking nonstop about a new bodybuilder at his gym. His nights had gotten longer. The days off disappeared. In his heart, Ledger had known he was cheating. He had truly hoped their twenty years together would win in the end. It seemed he never stood a chance. Ledger blinked, wishing the past would stop haunting his every waking moment. That had been seven years ago. He should be over it. Ledger was over it. It was the trauma and betrayal he couldn't shake—the way the entire bullshit had turned him bitter and made him automatically not trust anyone he met. Then Valon had vanished into the world of fame, leaving Ledger with nothing but the horrible person he became. It was lonely. He was lonely.

A light tap on his shoulder broke through the silent spiraling. "It's time."

At security's warning, he turned his head to tell Kash the plan. He found Kash's intense stare locked on him. While Kash was unreadable, Ledger's heart skipped a beat. He wasn't sure if it was fear or something else. Before he had time to decipher his feelings, Kash stood and immediately positioned himself where he could keep Ledger safe. It seemed Kash considered this a genuine job. One he took seriously and was obviously good at. As they headed to the green room, he swore he felt Kash on his heels. It felt strange, but at least he knew the person who would always be in his personal space now.

In an unlucky turn of events, he didn't even get a moment to speak with Kash before Valon came crashing through a different door. He looked high on adrenaline.

Valon was all smiles and childlike energy. "How was the show?"

Ledger didn't even sit. That was how on edge he was. "It was great. You always put on an amazing show. I'm proud of you."

Valon's gaze didn't look Kash's way for even a second. "I'm so glad you came tonight. It feels like forever since we've seen each other."

A nervous chuckle slipped from Ledger. "That's because it has been. You're too busy for me now."

Valon made a dismissive gesture and grabbed a bottle of water from an ice bucket on the table. "I bought you a friend. Bonus points, it's someone you know. You'll be good."

So he had known. His chest hurt so much, he wondered if he was having a heart attack. His son had bought him a friend. The entire situation was worse than he thought. "Ah. This entire thing has been about getting me off your back. I see."

Valon looked his way after chugging half the bottle. He rolled his eyes. "You act like I'm treating you like a kid or something. You went and made yourself internet famous. I have guards." He made a hand gesture in the complete opposite direction of where his guards stood. "It's part of the life."

Ledger wanted to scream and throw shit. He didn't even know this person standing in front of him. He had to change the subject. "Are you still good to spend the day with me tomorrow before you leave town?"

Valon eyed the drink selection after tossing his bottle in the direction of the trash. A guard grabbed it and tossed it in. "We'll see. Bond says at least three local news outlets have reached out for interviews. You know, the whole local-boy angle. I need to look that over."

Ledger pinched the spot between his eyes. It wasn't as if Valon looked at him anyway. There was no need for him to hide his aggravation.

The same door Valon had appeared through was thrown open. An obnoxious screamed growl cut through the air. Ledger's ears still rang from the concert, and that didn't stop him from cringing at the sound. Valon's drummer held up two bottles of expensive liquor.

Valon headed that way without looking back. "Yes! Thank fuck." He was gone before Ledger could ask a single question.

"Your car is here."

Ledger was closer to tears than he wanted to admit.

Strong hands squeezed his shoulders. "I'm sorry." The softly spoken words nearly pushed him over the edge. He didn't know whether he felt better or worse having Kash witness him losing his son. At least he wasn't going home alone. Maybe he needed a drink too.

Chapter Two

The trip from the concert venue to Ledger's home was one of the most heartbreaking rides Kash had ever taken. The silence tried to crush his ears. Ledger stared out the window. Occasionally, he would swipe his eyes, but he never once looked Kash's way. Kash shouldn't be here. While he would never hate himself for setting in motion pushing Valon to the top, he hadn't considered how much Ledger had lost in his absence.

To be fair, no way in hell had Kash predicted Valon would turn into that asshole he had just seen.

They pulled into the driveway of a house Kash would never have pictured Ledger living. It was massive for one person. He was willing to bet the place was a good eight thousand square feet. Fuck. He couldn't see Ledger milling around a house this big alone. That sounded miserable. Ledger was too down to earth for this. The space probably made his life feel empty as hell. At least, Kash hoped that was the case. Maybe Ledger had remarried or had a boyfriend living with him. For all he knew, Ledger might have step kids. All the confusion he had experienced before leaving town was rushing back.

Ledger straightened from his slouch and cleared his throat. "I guess this is where you're living now. When we get inside, I'll show you around. Just pick a room. It's just me. Besides my bedroom, no one else uses any of the other rooms. Plus, Valon had every inch of the place furnished like I would be hosting overnight galas or something. Are you hungry?"

He really was alone in the world. Kash had to lock down his mind. "I was starving when I got off the plane. Now I've kind of lost my appetite."

Ledger sniffed and met Kash's stare. He looked... empty. Kash didn't know how to explain that. "Sorry. I didn't think of asking any questions. Where are you coming from? I thought Steel Security was based here in California." He made a gesture as if wiping away the words. "Close by is what I should've said."

He didn't know how much he should say. Kash didn't want to have to keep up with lies. "They actually have offices all over the country, but taking this job was a favor to my cousin. I've been living in Atlantic City for about a year, working odd jobs."

"Your cousin?"

Kash nodded. "Steel."

"Well." Ledger climbed from the car and tipped the driver. He didn't speak again until they headed inside. "That clears up one thing. Valon would know that."

"Yeah." Kash dragged out the word. "His claim of buying me for you is total BS, by the way. Not only do I not work for Steel full time, but he had someone else lined up to take this job and it fell through. I volunteered to come since he was a man short on live-in bodyguards."

Ledger missed a step and spun. "You volunteered?"

A bright smile exploded across his face at Ledger's open shock. "To be fair, I didn't know it was you until I agreed to help."

"And you still came." It wasn't a question. Obviously, he came. Kash currently stood in Ledger's mudroom. Ledger looked right at him. He wouldn't be a smart-ass and point that out, though. Kash understood Ledger's stance. The way he left town was something only a man with no plans of ever looking back would do.

A sad smile tugged at Kash's lips as he stared into eyes that were a replica of the man Kash had thought he would spend the rest of his life with at one time in his life. "Of course I did. It's you."

For a moment, they simply held each other's stare. Finally, Ledger cleared his throat. "Do you want to order something to eat? I'm starved."

Kash fought the urge to rub his chest. Every second they were together felt wrong, but Kash wouldn't back down. "Sounds great."

With a dip of his chin, Ledger turned and led the way. "Would you like something to drink in the meantime?"

"Yeah. Point me in the right direction and I'll help. I mean, what the hell, Ledger?

This place is huge." With every second that passed, the more the years fell away.

Ledger made his way into the kitchen. Kash wanted to look in every direction. He needed to make a security plan. Kash's gaze wouldn't budge from Ledger. Ledger flashed an embarrassed-looking smile. "Valon. I guess this is how he makes himself feel better about forgetting I exist."

Kash hated that. "What's Ry's house look like?" He wasn't being an asshole. Kash knew Valon. He had a very good idea of how Ledger would answer, but he knew saying the words out loud would brighten Ledger's night.

Ledger snorted out a laugh. The sound made Kash smile. Ledger snagged two glasses and a chilled bottle of wine.

"From my understanding, he's living in an apartment at the back of his gym, which is a thing I didn't know existed." Ledger poured two glasses, keeping his eyes locked on his task. "I guess that's how he got away with cheating for so long."

Kash hated Ry. He always had. The guy had always been a shady son of a bitch who treated Valon like shit. Apparently, Ledger hadn't been getting loved properly either.

A hint of wickedness stoked inside Kash. He wasn't the sad fucker Valon had reduced him to being. Kash had moved on and turned into a whore. Self-proclaimed, of course. Kash grabbed a glass. "It's always been his loss. You're still just as sexy as you've ever been, and you've always been hot as fuck." Kash wandered away to inspect the room. He didn't wait to see Ledger's reaction. Kash had questions he needed answered before settling in for the night. If Ledger kept distracting him just by being himself, Kash would never learn why he was there. Kash had to keep Ledger safe. No one else ever had. Kash didn't mind taking the job. Ledger deserved that much.

Through a quick tour and sharing dinner, Ledger couldn't quiet his mind. Kash was a grown man. Even in his teenage years, Kash had been an adult. There had been many nights when they sat together and talked while Valon tried his best to juggle college and a budding music career. Kash hadn't been given the same advantages in life as Valon. Neither Kash nor Ledger slept well. He supposed they had equally carried too much stress from being unwanted by the people who claimed to love them. Kash had an alcoholic mom and a dad who had been long gone since childhood. He had been the stable one. The man of the house who raised himself. At seventeen, Kash's mom finally drank herself to death. As far as Ledger knew, Kash had never cried or mourned. He simply used the money he had saved from working every gig he could and cremated her. No one even noticed an underage boy living alone. He just endured the years afterward. Then, Valon had started college, and the first signs of Valon leaving Kash behind had started. Ledger had lost his husband. He supposed Kash had lost everything. They never spoke about those things. Honestly, Ledger couldn't even remember what they used to talk about. While Kash had changed in looks, and he had obviously gained a ton of confidence along with bitterness, he felt the same to Ledger. He didn't want to go to bed.

Kash didn't bring up the reason he was needed until they sat on opposite sides of the couch, turned sideways to face each other. They nursed their wine and let their food settle. Ledger felt way too cozy for Kash to talk business, but it was inevitable.

"Tell me why you need a guard. I need all the details so I can protect you."

Ledger had been vehemently opposed to this entire thing. Now he felt kind of warm inside at the idea of someone wanting to keep him safe. "Well." Ledger leaned over and set his glass on the coffee table before getting settled again. "After everyone disappeared into their lives, and Valon bought me this humongous house, I needed a distraction. Since Ry basically left with nothing but his clothes, all his books on nutrition and health coaching sat on the shelves. Don't ask me why I moved those things here. It just felt easier at the time. Then I got sick of looking at them, and pulled them off the shelf one day, intending to donate them. But a tagline caught my eye, and I ended up reading every book instead."

"What was the tagline?" Kash sounded genuinely curious.

"Maybe you're the problem."

Kash's eyebrows rose.

Ledger pushed on, hoping to zip through the embarrassing parts. "Anyhow, I used what I learned to create a meal plan. Then I moved on to coming up with recipes that allowed me to eat enough to actually feel full. One night, I had a date, and I cooked. The meal turned out great even though the date didn't. However, while the guy ate, he said I should share my recipes. They'd be a hit online." Kash shrugged. "I'd never spent much time on social media, but I made some videos just for the hell of it. Since I didn't have many followers, I just did my thing as always. I'd work out, shower, and then make a video while I cooked. One night, I spilled hot marinara on my shirt. It hurt like hell, so I quickly peeled off my shirt and tossed it away. I was doing a live, so I didn't think much about it. It's not like I could choose not to upload the video, so I just laughed off the whole thing."

"You blew up the moment they caught sight of that sexy body, didn't you?"

Heat exploded through Ledger's face. He hated that he blushed. "Yeah. It got seriously out of hand. The next thing I knew, all my videos went viral. I gained hundreds of thousands of followers overnight. The private messages hit immediately. Pictures and vivid paragraphs about what they would do to me. But with all of that, there also came the rape threats and death threats. At first, I just deleted them and blocked each person. Unfortunately, letters showed up, proving everyone knew where I lived. Worse, people approached me everywhere I went and showed up at my door. Gifts were left in the mailbox with no idea of where they came from. I already had a great security system, but it can only help so much. Valon started mentioning private security every time we spoke. I refused. No one wants to feel uncomfortable in their own home, living with a stranger. Then he just hired Steel Security, no matter my feelings on the matter, and here you are."

Kash nodded along while he sipped wine. "Tell me about your security system."

He was a familiar face who asked professional questions. Ledger relaxed a little more each second that passed. "Every entry and window are wired. The back door, coming in from the garage, has a minute delay when it's opened to give me time to turn it off before it calls the monitoring company. I always shut the door, disarm, and rearm. It's a habit now."

Kash's gaze sharpened. "I didn't see you do any of that when we came in." He dropped his feet to the floor and set his glass on the table. "You gave me the tour, but I should search the place."

Ledger couldn't stop smiling. Kash took keeping him safe seriously, and it was nice. "I disarmed with the key fob since we came through a door with no delay. Admittedly, in doing it that way, and with you distracting me, I didn't reset it. I should do that."

Kash stood. "Show me the system."

Since Ledger's keys were in the kitchen and the unit was by the door closest to the kitchen, he headed that way. He still felt every step Kash made behind him. For some reason, Ledger was highly aware of every move Kash made. It wasn't unnerving exactly. His mind simply refused to budge from Kash.

Ledger made his way to the door that led to the garage. He motioned toward the keypad. “That’s it.”

Kash looked it over.

“Oh.” Ledger moved closer. “I should create a code for you, since you live here now, or you could just use mine. It’s up to you.”

“You can just give me yours and save some hassle.”

Ledger nodded. That was easier, especially since he wasn’t a hundred percent sure he remembered how to add another person into the system. “Let me see your phone. I’ll add myself to your contacts with my number, alarm PIN, and the address here. Then you should be set.”

Kash motioned toward the kitchen. "I left my phone on the counter."

Together they stepped into the kitchen. Kash grabbed the device, unlocked it, and then handed the phone to Ledger. Ledger went straight to the contacts. He tried not to think about Kash's blank wallpaper. Maybe he read too much into a small thing, but the wallpaper on people's phones was a popular avenue for expressing oneself or showcasing someone they love. Kash had a black background, devoid of life.

While Ledger typed, a text message flashed across the screen. *We have a quick job if you have time.* There was nothing inherently bad in the message. For whatever reason, a gut feeling hit. Kash just seemed so hardened. Dangerous.

Ledger finished and passed the device back. "A text came through while I was typing my info."

Kash nodded and shoved the phone into his back pocket without looking at the device, obviously giving no fucks about any messages. "It's nearly two a.m. I guess I should pick one of those rooms."

Ledger nodded, even as a sense of sadness overcame him. He hadn't sat and spoken with anyone in a while. While Ledger was tired, he already knew he wouldn't sleep. Ledger made his way down the hall. He motioned toward the path they walked. "Pick any one of these."

"Which is closest to you?"

Ledger had to hide his emotions before he turned and met Kash's stare. "There's a guest room next to mine, but it's tiny.

The bathroom is basically just a small sink, walk-in shower, and a toilet. These rooms are a lot bigger with much better bathrooms."

Kash never broke eye contact. "The one next to you. I can't keep you safe at night if I can't hear you shout."

That made sense. Ledger still felt bad, though. Kash deserved a better room.

"Come on." Ledger brushed past him and headed in the opposite direction. Kash was such a big guy, Ledger had to turn sideways to scoot past him. If he wasn't mistaken, Kash intentionally forced Ledger to touch him. Maybe he was losing his mind. When he reached Kash's new bedroom and the lights flared to life, a major detail hit Ledger. As Kash strolled into the bedroom, Ledger couldn't believe he hadn't noticed sooner. "You don't have any luggage."

Kash eyed the room. He didn't meet Ledger's stare. "The airport lost my bags."

Ledger shook his head. "Why didn't you say something? We could've made a quick trip to buy what you need until your bags are found. There's nothing open now." As he spoke, Ledger realized it wasn't just the bags. Kash hadn't spoken much at all. He hadn't told Ledger anything of value about his life now. Kash had spent the night asking questions and focusing on Ledger. Ledger hadn't even noticed the deflection.

"I'm good. Tomorrow, I'll get a car and pick up whatever I need. It's not a big deal. It's not like I'll sleep anyway. Tomorrow will be here soon enough."

Ledger had never wanted to stay put so badly in his life. He wanted to hear Kash's every story. "I have a pair of pajama pants you can borrow. Everything you need to shower is in the bathroom. If you can't find what you need, I'll probably have something you can use. I want you to feel like this is your home."

The intensity of Kash's stare had Ledger holding his breath. "This place already feels closer to home than any place I've lived in years. You're here."

Ledger swallowed. He had to be reading too much into Kash's every word. They had known each other for a long time. That was all. It had to be all.

"Well, I'm not going anywhere, so... would you like those pants?"

A smile lit Kash's face. His eyes twinkled with silent laughter. "Yeah. I want your pants."

There was so much humor in Kash's tone, Ledger couldn't help but smile. This was the Kash he remembered. He was steady, serious, and kind, but he was also playful with a slightly wicked sense of humor. Damn.

"I've really missed you." Even though Ledger kind of wanted to bite off his tongue, he didn't take his words back. He had a feeling Kash needed someone to miss him.

"Me too."

The funny thing was, Ledger didn't know which of them Kash meant. Ledger had a bad feeling it was himself.

Chapter Three

Kash stared at the dark bedroom ceiling, wearing Ledger's pants. He couldn't stop over-analyzing every second he spent with Ledger. All the nights he heard Ledger pace, and Kash had joined him, ran through his mind. They had never spoken about anything heavy. Yet, somehow, he had also told Ledger every ugly detail of his home life. Ledger had never judged him or acted like he would call CPS. He understood Kash took care of himself, and life in the system would be worse than powering through a couple of months. It wasn't like he had been physically abused or anything. His mom had just checked out long before she died. No big deal. A lot of people had worse problems than he did—like Ledger. Ledger had a cheating husband who loved tormenting his son. Of course, it had made perfect sense for Ry to leave on Valon's eighteenth birthday. The possibility of paying child support had kept him trapped in a marriage he didn't want anymore. Except there were real people hurting from his every shitty move. While he knew Ledger suspected Ry slept around, he had never found definitive proof. Kash knew that because he knew Ledger. Ledger wasn't weak, and he had a backbone of steel. If he could have proven he wasn't simply crazy—at least according to Ry, who called him that all the time—Ledger would have kicked his ass to the curb. But Ledger wasn't the type to throw away a twenty-year marriage over a gut feeling. Unfortunately, Kash had known Ledger's suspicions were true. Not only had Kash stalked Ry until he found the truth, but Ry had also propositioned Kash a time or two. Kash was two years older than Valon and had graduated two years ahead of him. After he walked across that stage he never thought he would conquer, Kash stole a bottle of Jack from his mom and went home with Valon to get absolutely shitfaced. When he heard quiet steps moving through the house, Kash immediately climbed out of bed to sit with Ledger. Except it wasn't Ledger, and Ry had been way too welcoming. That encounter had shaken Kash a bit, especially since it turned out to be the first in a long line of uncomfortable nights. While he stayed at Valon's place more than his own home, he wasn't allowed to sleep in the same bed as Valon. They had given Kash a bedroom—very likely due to Ledger worrying about his safety at home. No matter the reason, Kash had been alone and unprotected each night as he slept. After that night, Kash had started working on beefing up his muscles and sleeping with a gun. The piece had been his dad's, and Kash had hung on to it for years to keep it from his mom's drunken hands. Kash had to teach himself how to use the gun, but he had never possessed any qualms about murdering that rat bastard if pushed. Thankfully, Ry never tipped

Kash's hand. That was good because, as it turned out, Kash didn't own a single ounce of remorse or reluctance when it came to killing anyone at all. Maybe he was a psychopath. It was possible life had simply broken Kash. No matter the reason, Kash was completely unmoved by the light leaving someone's eyes. A lot of people were better off dead. Ry was one of those people.

A thought hit, distracting Kash from his Ledger musings. Honestly, it wasn't too late for Kash to take out that target. Unfortunately, that wouldn't change the past, and Ledger might look at him differently. That would kill Kash. Until he set eyes on Ledger tonight, Kash hadn't remembered the full extent of his heartbreak. He thought the hurt had eased. It turned out the trauma had just gotten easier to carry. Now he remembered everything, and Kash hated it. Well, he hated Ry. But that was—

Kash's thoughts died a swift death. A bright light lit his ceiling from outside, and a shadow crossed. Kash was out of bed in a flash. Like a total dumbass, he hadn't secured a weapon yet. He thought it could wait until morning. Now he saw how wrong he had been. He jetted down the hall.

Ledger was right behind him. "What's happened?"

Kash didn't look back. He needed every ounce of focus to keep Ledger safe. "There's someone outside. Go to your room, lock the door, and don't turn your back on the window. If you've got a gun, get it now." Kash didn't bother looking to see if he had been obeyed. He yanked open the first door he came to that led him outside. His eyes were already adjusted to the dark. The floodlights were on, but Kash's gaze swept the area they missed. Someone was there. Kash felt them. The last wisps of clothing turned the corner, as if someone darted out of sight. He ran after them. Sharp rocks dug into his bare feet. He stubbed his toe on something that was part of the landscaping. Fuck, he really needed a better look at the place. In his defense, he hadn't thought anyone could hurt Ledger.

As the dark shadow came into sight, Kash dove, tackling the trespasser and taking them to the ground.

"Holy shit! What the fuck?"

Wait, Kash recognized that aggravated voice. He flipped the man beneath him. It was Valon. He smelled as if he had bathed in liquor, and he looked exactly how Kash's mother had looked every time she disappeared inside a bottle.

"Kash? Why are you on top of me? Not that I'm complaining, but I'll probably feel that in the morning." He was beyond calm. Valon sounded bored.

Kash stood, pulling Valon to his feet with him. "Why are you lurking around outside? Where are your guards?"

Valon swiped at his clothing and didn't meet Kash's eyes. "They quit, and I'm here to crash. I forgot the front door doesn't have a delay. When I remembered, I circled the house to come in through the garage."

The alarm hadn't gone off when Kash yanked it open. Why? He had seen Ledger arm the system. Kash focused on what he could. "How did you even get here?"

Valon headed for the garage without looking to see if Kash followed. "My manager." He headed inside, basically ignoring Kash from that point. Valon moved down the hall and went inside the first room he came to. The door closed with a snap behind him.

Kash rolled his eyes and closed all the doors left open. He set the alarm before lightly knocking on Ledger's bedroom door.

"All clear."

Ledger opened the door. He didn't look scared, only worried. "Everything good?"

Kash almost hated to tell him. “Yeah. It was Valon, stumbling around drunk as fuck and trying to find a way inside.”

Ledger blinked. “Valon is here?”

Kash nodded. “First room on the left down the second hallway.”

Ledger didn’t look happy or relieved. His every mannerism screamed he was divided. Ledger shifted from one foot to the other.

Kash fought for his life to stop himself from dropping his gaze to Ledger’s bare chest. They were the same height. He couldn’t check out Ledger’s body without Ledger noticing, but wow. No wonder Ledger had the world in an uproar.

“I’ll let him sleep it off.”

Kash had forgotten what they talked about.

"At least he's here and not dead in a back alley somewhere."

Oh, yeah. Valon. He was Ledger's son. Ledger was old enough to be his father. Damn, he didn't look it. Kash nodded along with everything Ledger said. Valon was long forgotten.

After a moment, silence penetrated his thoughts. Kash realized they stood in the doorway and stared at each other. Someone needed to break the heaviness that grew in the air.

Kash cleared his throat. "I guess I should get back to bed and let you get some sleep."

Ledger took a step back. "Yeah, you need to rest too. You've had a long day."

Kash got his first decent look at Ledger's bedroom. It looked cozy yet manly. His gaze moved to Ledger's soft-looking bed. It was high and covered with thick blankets. The room was freezing, and a book sat on the bed. It was in Kash's nature to be observant. Keeping his eyes and feet moving kept him alive.

He took a step back. "Goodnight, Ledger." Saying his name was totally unnecessary. The name simply rolled from his tongue, sounding like a loving caress. Kash had to walk away. He wasn't above fucking his ex's dad. His moral compass stopped working a long time ago. He couldn't disrespect Ledger, though. Ledger was special. Kash wouldn't forget that.

Ledger stared at his closed bedroom door, seeing nothing. The way Kash said his name still rang in his ears. There was something sitting on his chest. Sadness like he hadn't felt in years engulfed him. He turned. His empty bed waited for him. Ledger's gaze skipped away from the depressing sight. He faced the door again. Maybe he should grab an entire bottle of wine and send himself into oblivion—as his son had done. Ledger's feet didn't budge. The way Kash's mom had always done. He didn't want to become that person. But Ledger couldn't make his feet move toward the bed. His throat swelled. He felt emptier than he had in years. Any second, his heart would stop from the pressure closing in on him. His vision darkened at the edges. The door flew open.

Kash stood in the open doorway, looking furious. "Well, now I can't fucking sleep." He grabbed Ledger's hand and towed him toward the bed. "It's time for bed. If I can't stay here, and see for myself you're fine, I'll never get any goddamn rest."

His open fury brought a smile to Ledger's lips and lifted the invisible weight suffocating him. "You need your sleep. Like I said, it's been a long day for you." Ledger had to stay focused on Kash's health and not the fact they would be under the same covers.

Kash shot him an irritated look that had Ledger pressing his lips together to keep from laughing. "Quit thinking about everyone else first." The words were gruff and sent chills down Ledger's spine. He felt younger than he had in years. Ridiculously, Ledger wanted to get in bed and kick his feet like a little kid. Kash's presence just brought out something in him. Something unnamed he hadn't felt in years.

Ledger dutifully climbed into bed.

Kash turned out the lights and got into bed next to him.

For a moment, they were flat on their backs and equally silent. At the same time, they rolled to face each other. Kash's eyes shone eerily bright in the darkness, especially since he openly stared at Ledger.

"Did you mean it when you said you missed me?"

Kash's voice soothed something inside Ledger where no one could see. The darkness engulfing them made the moment feel intimate.

"Yes. It just hit me like a wave while we were standing there. All the times we stayed up talking kind of hit me all at once. When Valon and you split, I kind of went off at him over the situation."

"I heard. He texted me to tell me how horrible I am for turning the only father he has left against him. So I disappeared.

You're his dad. I'm nobody. I couldn't put you in the middle."

A sad smile tugged at Ledger's lips. "Technically, I put myself in the middle. While I understand all the valid reasons you two had to go separate ways, Valon wasn't the only one who lost you, and I was still at the height of dealing with my own bullshit. I projected onto him, and that was a failing I'll always have to live with. That's not on you. You loved him, and you were one of the steadiest parts of his life. It broke my heart to watch you two fall apart, especially since I knew you were the person who kept him grounded. Now look at him."

Kash didn't respond right away. In the silence, Ledger began to regret the confession. His speech sounded a little too much like he blamed Kash for who Valon had become. That was not what he meant, and Ledger didn't know how to fix it.

Kash's foot lightly brushed his beneath the covers, taking away every panic that slowly built. "You're a good person. Someday Valon will come back down to reality. It's inevitable. One day, he'll wake up, look around, and realize he pushed away everyone who truly loved him, leaving him with nothing but fake people who use him and leave him empty. I'm not trying to make you feel worse. Sometimes, people have to learn lessons the hard way. All you can do is keep showing up, proving you'll always be here, waiting to welcome him back."

Ledger was uncomfortably close to tears. When he spoke, he barely managed to get above a whisper. "You'll never understand how much I hate how life taught you way too many lessons too soon. You deserved to get to have your shithead years too."

A smile exploded across Kash's face. "Don't worry. I've gotten my bad boy era. It's been pretty epic."

"Then you came home to where you always knew I'd be waiting." Ledger didn't know why he had said that. Worse, he wasn't sure he meant it in a fatherly way. Kash had always felt older than his years to Ledger. He had always felt more like a friend than he should have. But maybe they had needed each other, as horrifying as that sounded to him. Maybe they still needed each other. A family neither of them had. Except he didn't feel like family in that moment.

Kash spoke quietly. His entire demeanor changed. His voice sounded exactly like a man ready to bare all his secrets. "Real talk. I stopped letting myself think about you a long time ago."

That stung. "I suppose that's fair."

Kash's foot brushed his again. "It's not on you. If I let myself think about those last three months, when Valon left to go on tour and never so much as texted me the entire time, I'd have to face a harsh truth."

Ledger's breathing shallowed. He wondered if he would faint from how honed in he was on every word Kash spoke. He was torn between needing to know and being scared he already knew. "What truth?" He shouldn't have asked, but goddamn it. Ledger needed to hear the words.

"Maybe—in the end—I wasn't as innocent in our breakup as I wanted to believe. I knew if I looked too closely, I'd have to admit I wished you were mine."

Tears unexpectedly clogged his throat. He couldn't respond. Reality tore him in two directions.

"It's okay if you want that new guard now."

Slight panic hit. He couldn't let Kash believe that was what he wanted. "No. You're the one I want." God help him. Ledger couldn't say he hadn't meant the words in every way possible. Kash had him all the way fucked up. He wasn't sure he cared to stop.

"We should get some sleep."

"Yeah." Kash's agreement sounded gruff.

Ledger couldn't take it. His hand found Kash's beneath the covers. Their fingers linked. As if that was all they needed, their eyes closed. The exhaustion won.

Chapter Four

With his mind intentionally blank, Ledger moved around the kitchen. He cooked breakfast while wearing nothing but pajama pants and an apron. With people in the house, Ledger wanted to make his video for this week's upload before he had witnesses. Alone, doing these cooking lessons didn't seem as embarrassing. Knowing someone could watch him in real life was mortifying.

He chopped peppers for omelets, explaining as he went. "You can use as many or as few peppers as you like. Peppers are packed with vitamins, antioxidants, and fiber." Ledger tossed the peppers into the skillet. With his mind on lockdown, Ledger talked through the process, fully focused on the task and ensuring he didn't miss any vital steps. Finally, he showed off the finished product. After taking a bite, he said his goodbyes and ended the recording.

A low chuckle rumbled through the room. "You really are the internet's silver daddy, aren't you?"

A hot blush exploded across Ledger's face as Kash strolled into the room. He also wore only the pajama pants Ledger loaned him. Ledger bit back a groan. He didn't know how long Kash had watched him. "Since my hair started to gray when I was nineteen, I might as well use it to my advantage."

Kash pulled out a stool at the kitchen island and sat. His gaze moved over Ledger's face. Ledger knew what he saw. Solid white hair and beard, groomed and styled to be presentable for the world.

Ledger didn't look away. He was too curious to see any reaction Kash showed. He didn't get the chance.

Valon appeared from the hall. "I thought I smelled food." He pulled out the stool next to Kash and sat.

Ledger's throat swelled, seeing the pair so close to each other again. A scalding wave of jealousy washed over him before the massive guilt took over. Valon was his son. Kash was his ex. Ledger was a bad person.

Valon's gaze swept over them, obviously taking in the way they were dressed. He went back to focusing on the food. “It’s your famous omelet. Cool.”

Ledger set his plate in front of Valon. “You can have this one. I’ll throw together more. How are you feeling this morning?” He did his damnedest to act like it was a typical morning. He knew Kash was right. One day, likely sooner rather than later with the way Valon partied, he would need a soft place to land when he fell. That place should be with Ledger.

Valon dug into the food and talked as he ate. “I’m good. Just another after-concert celebration. I bounce back pretty quickly.”

It hit Ledger. Valon's voice sounded horrible—like his throat hurt. He quickly poured Valon some coffee and doctored it to his liking. "Here. Drink this. Hopefully, the heat will ease your throat. Are you sure you're good?"

"Yep." Valon took a drink and went back to eating.

Ledger took a chance and sneaked a quick peek in Kash's direction. He had to tear his gaze away. Kash was intensely focused on him—like Valon wasn't even there.

Valon bumped shoulders with Kash. "Thanks for that public appearance last night. If you'd come through the back way, I would've missed an opportunity to have everyone talking today. Extra coverage is always a good thing."

"Sure thing. What are ex-best friends for?"

The unbothered note in Kash's voice had Ledger looking Kash's way again. By all accounts, there was no reason for Kash to put up with Valon's antics. Kash looked as unmoved as he sounded. While Ledger looked on, Kash stood, and circled the island to pour a cup of coffee for himself. The silence in the room was unnerving.

Ledger went to work on two more omelets to give himself somewhere to focus his attention. There was way too much spinning around inside his head. In the end, Ledger knew he had to take advantage of the time Valon gave him.

He focused on his son. "Have you decided whether we can spend the day together?"

Valon looked slightly panicked.

Ledger barely stopped himself from groaning. He knew what came next, and he was right.

"Did we make plans for today?"

Ledger took a calming breath. "Yes. Several times, actually. Each time you reiterated, you would be free."

Valon sat there for a moment, as if searching his mind. Finally, he shrugged. "Oops. I have interviews all day. Maybe tonight after I'm done, if you're still up. For now, you have Kash. You've always liked his company better than mine anyhow. You'll be good."

For a moment, Ledger just stared at Valon. He tried hanging on to Kash's advice. Ledger wanted any part of his son he could get. Unfortunately, he hit his limit. “Okay. I’m done.” He walked away, leaving everything behind, including eggs that were likely burning now. The bedroom door closed behind him in a snap. He needed a hot shower. Ledger felt numb. He had to keep his mind on lockdown. If he looked at things too closely now, Ledger might walk away from everything in his life. Ry had made it look easy. Maybe he had the right idea.

Kash did his best to finish cooking the breakfast Ledger had started. He counted backwards from a hundred inside his head. Valon didn't know him any longer. He didn't see the monster Kash had become. If Kash snapped, it might not be a screaming match. It was well past time someone should have talked to Valon with their fists. The scrawny ass wouldn't survive that kind of matchup with him. Plus, he wouldn't hurt Ledger like that.

He loved this son who didn't deserve him.

"You can say whatever it is you're thinking. Pretty soon you won't have any enamel left on your teeth from grinding them so hard."

Kash dumped the omelet on a plate without bothering to look at Valon. "Why? You know you're being a shitty person. Like always, nothing I say to you will matter."

A heartbeat of silence passed before Valon responded. He sounded every bit as unmoved as Kash expected. "He took your side, you know. Against his own son," he added as if the gravity of his first statement hadn't gotten the reaction he wanted. So he chose a fight they'd already had.

Kash finally met his stare. He let Valon see the man he dealt with now. "I never would've asked that of him. We made our choices with open eyes. If that's why you're treating your dad like garbage, that's childish as fuck. For real. I used to think nothing could make me think badly of you. If you're treating Ledger like shit over a guy you thought of as dead weight, then wow. That's as pathetic as it gets, dude."

Kash grabbed the plate he had made along with some silverware. He followed Ledger's path down the hall without looking back. Nothing mattered anymore anyhow. Valon was the huge star he always dreamed of being. Kash was a nomad with a large, ill-gotten bank account. Ledger was the silver daddy he should be. All three of them were on widely different paths. Kash didn't need anyone. He never had.

Kash knocked on Ledger's bedroom door. When no one answered, he peeked inside. Steam rolled from the open bathroom door. Kash stared at the doorway for much longer than intended. Fuck it. He was a bad person. No need to pretend otherwise. Kash stepped inside the room and closed the door behind him. There was an accent chair in the corner with a small round table next to it. Kash had to push the lamp to the edge to make room for Ledger's plate. The eggs would be as cold as ice before Ledger got around to eating them. He had barely gotten settled before a soft knock tapped on the door. Valon was the only other person there. Kash froze. He didn't think it would be a great idea for Valon to know

Kash was inside his dad's bedroom. He stayed put, hoping Valon wouldn't open the door. When a minute passed with no more knocking, he chanced a peek out the door. No one was there, but a fresh omelet and their abandoned coffees sat at the door. Kash looked right and left before carrying the items into the room. He grabbed the cold plate for himself and left the hot one for Ledger. Kash sat back and ate, wondering what the hell was going on with Valon. Why would he bring their coffees and leave them together? Was he making a statement? Did he think Kash was fucking his dad? Was this a passive-aggressive move? Goddamn it. He hated the way he felt in this town. Always had. Kash should have let Steel assign someone else to this job. Drama averted. All these old feelings would have stayed buried in the shallow grave he had left them in. Everything closed in around him. He felt like that angry, helpless teen who carried the weight of the world again. To some extent, pushing Valon toward fame was Kash living vicariously through him. Kash had known he would never be anything, but Valon would. Now look at them. Ledger had been abandoned by everyone he loved. Kash was filled with bitterness and didn't care what happened to him. Valon was... something. Kash hadn't quite figured that one out yet.

Ledger stepped out of the bathroom and froze. Water ran down his torso, soaked away by the towel around Ledger's hips. The unadulterated lust that slapped Kash nearly broke his thin civil veneer. He never even thought about Valon anymore, but this. This was something he sweated and twisted in the sheets for many a night. Kash couldn't look away. He didn't have the strength.

However, Kash could try to make things less awkward. "I have breakfast. You need fortification for the day I have planned." There was no hiding the innuendo. He wanted things. Kash had wanted things for a long damn time.

Ledger cleared his throat and grabbed a robe from the bed. He pulled on the robe before subtly dropping the towel from underneath.

Kash hid a smile. Ledger knew he was being hunted.

With his dignity restored, Ledger crossed the room. He eyed the plate that had been left for him. "Thank you."

Kash tapped the empty plate he held with his fork. “I made this one. Valon made that one. It might still be lukewarm.”

Ledger’s gorgeous gaze moved from the plate to Kash. “Valon made this?”

Kash shrugged. “Maybe it’s an olive branch or whatever.” Kash stood. “Here. Take the chair.” While Ledger sat, Kash rearranged the coffee mugs, so Ledger’s was closer. “There. Breakfast of champions.”

Ledger’s smile made the ridiculous statement worthwhile. “So what do you have planned for the day?”

Kash sat on the bench at the end of the bed. “Like you said, I need to replace my stuff. If you have a shirt or something I can borrow, I'll just wear my jeans from yesterday."

Ledger pointed his fork toward a nearby door. "Check the closet. Take whatever you need."

Kash needed the distraction. Ledger was too close and wore too little. He headed into the closet. It was huge. There was a lot of stuff inside, especially shoes.

Kash chuckled as he stuck his head out the door. "I never would've pegged you as a shoe hoarder."

A hint of embarrassment crossed Ledger's face. "Don't judge me. I have my vices."

Kash laughed as he dove back in. He grabbed a shoe and checked the size. "Uh oh. We wear the same size shoes. You're in trouble now. I'm a thief." Kash was only half joking. He found pants and a shirt in his size. Kash stripped off the pajama pants Ledger had loaned him. He would do a load of laundry later.

Something shifted in the air.

Kash turned.

Ledger stood in the doorway. He didn't look away. There were no blushes now. "Sorry. You got quiet, so I came to help. I guess you don't need me after all."

Kash held Ledger's stare. He wanted to crack a joke and lighten the mood. That didn't happen. Kash opened his mouth, and the truth fell out. "I'm pretty sure I'll always need you." Kash was a tad mortified. He hadn't meant to say that. Kash struggled to move on. "Now that I know we're the same size, I can just wear everything you own and wait for my luggage."

"You're not doing that." Ledger sounded calm. In control. "I'm taking you shopping." He stepped inside the closet, invading Kash's space as he reached for an outfit behind him. They were so close. Kash was rock hard. The moment Ledger gave him an inch to breathe, Kash pulled on the borrowed pants with lightning quickness before he embarrassed them both. It was painful zipping his erection behind the tight jeans.

Ledger did not make it easier. His robe fell open, and Kash was treated to the full show. Damn. *Yum*. Unfortunately, Ledger dressed too quickly for Kash to enjoy watching for long.

With an inner sigh, Kash pulled on the t-shirt. The moment his head poked through the hole, their gazes met. What he saw in Ledger's eyes nearly brought him to his knees. He felt everything Kash did, and Kash wasn't sure if Ledger would ever admit it. For the millionth time in Kash's life, he was literally inches from a beautiful dream. As always, there was no chance of it coming true.

Chapter Five

DAMN. THAT WAS ALL Ledger could think. Just, damn. Kash did all the right things, very obviously working as Ledger's bodyguard. Yet somehow Ledger also spent the day with his friend. It became immediately apparent Kash could afford anything he wanted. It was a tad unnerving, considering he had no idea what odd jobs Kash did when he wasn't keeping people safe. Ledger couldn't think of a tactful way to ask. Kash spent fifteen hundred dollars without blinking, including two new pairs of shoes for Ledger. Ledger had argued vehemently over that one. Kash had simply walked to the counter and paid for them while completely ignoring Ledger. He had used a debit card for every purchase. Ledger finally broke when they sat down inside a restaurant for lunch.

"Okay. You've spent a ton of money today and have plans to spend more before the day—"

While still staring at the menu, Kash cut him off. "Don't ask something you'll regret."

For a full minute, Ledger stared at Kash's profile. For nowhere near the first time, Ledger thought about Kash's hard body, the scars he had seen when he walked in on Kash changing, and Kash's overall demeanor now. He had to know. "Is it drugs?"

A bright smile exploded across Kash's face. His eyes danced with laughter as they focused on Ledger. He was breathtaking. "I'm sorry. I know it's not funny, but the way you asked that was hilarious. 'Is it drugs?' You sound like one of those dads in commercials."

The way Kash mimicked him was pretty damn funny. Maybe he needed to lighten up. Truthfully, if he were Kash, he would be offended that anyone's mind went to drugs first. Just because Kash had a hard life, that didn't mean he fell into anything shady. "Sorry."

Kash shook his head, still smiling like an idiot. "Don't be. It is drugs." Kash obviously gave no fucks about Ledger's shock. He just kept talking. "Well, partly. I've also been sent to shake down money from people who owe debts and worse. There's a whole world of underground crime, and I've done every job I've been hired to do. The last few years have been a ride."

"Please tell me you're joking." Even Ledger heard the way he held very little hope it was a tall tale.

Kash was entirely serious and unashamed. His lack of worry showed in every line of his body. "No. You'd be amazed at what you'll do when you don't care about anything, and you have nothing to lose. Most of my life, I haven't had much of anything tethering me to this world. So..." He shrugged again and went back to reading the menu.

Ledger wasn't fooled. Kash said one thing, but the way he gripped his hands into fists and the focus he visibly forced on what the restaurant had to offer said a lot. He might not have anything to lose. Kash very well might not give a single damn what happened to him, but he cared what Ledger thought. He had ripped off a Band-Aid and exposed himself, expecting rejection.

Ledger searched his heart. At the end of the day, he knew Kash. Kash was an amazing human. And what had Ledger expected, really? Kash had disappeared into a harsh world with no money and only a high school diploma to his name. Life hadn't given him many choices, and Kash hadn't lied. Kash had nothing to lose. He expected everything to hurt. Ledger couldn't be on that list.

He picked up his menu and flipped it open. “Honestly, that’s kind of hot.” Ledger kept his gaze glued to lunch offerings. He never wanted to know Kash’s reaction, but he felt the way Kash’s stare bored into him. Ledger waited until he saw Kash look down before he sneaked a peek. Kash was back to being completely unreadable. Ledger hated it.

“You only look at me when you think I’m not paying attention.” Kash’s gaze lifted and collided with Ledger’s stare. He was too intense for Ledger to look away. “Why?”

Ledger took the question seriously. Kash deserved the same honesty he always gave Ledger, no matter the outcome. “I don’t know.”

Kash still never broke eye contact. "I know I've changed. It's not like I'm unaware of who I am now. Is it because I scare you?"

Ledger had never been more lost in someone's eyes. Kash was an eerily deep person. Ledger wanted to dive in. "No. At least, I'm not frightened in the way I think you mean."

"Keep talking." The hungry growl in Kash's voice had Ledger's body on fire.

"It's—"

"Thank fucking Christ. You're worse than a teen. I had to follow your location on the family app to find you."

The entire restaurant went silent as Valon loudly dragged a chair to their table and sat. He had two bodyguards in tow. Kash obviously recognized one. They nodded at each other in greeting.

The pair kept Valon blocked in, securing him from anyone who wanted to rush him. Valon was a huge celebrity. He would be lucky if they weren't mobbed, but Ledger was glad to see him.

A waitress appeared from thin air and handed Valon a menu. "Can I get you something to drink?" No one else at the table existed.

"Iced tea."

"Right away."

Valon wore sunglasses and never looked the woman's way. "I haven't eaten here in years. Is the menu even the same?"

Ledger was fucking flabbergasted. Valon never showed up. Was it because Kash was here? Did he want him back? A pain sliced through him at the thought. Ledger needed to take a huge step back. He had let himself forget who Kash was.

He swallowed the growing hurt. "Um. We just sat down. I haven't had time to check. I don't think I've eaten here either since the last time we came."

"It was my birthday, right? I don't remember which." Valon moved his sunglasses from his face to his head as he asked the question. His eyes were surprisingly clear.

"I'm old. Don't count on me to remember."

A bright smile lit Valon's face. A weight lifted from Ledger's chest. It was the first time Ledger had seen his real son in years. He kind of wanted to cry.

"You're not old, Dad. You had to get a bodyguard to save you from the crowd of people tripping over themselves to get a piece of you. It's too soon for you to play that card."

Ledger couldn't stop smiling. "It's good to see you. You've been gone too long." He absolutely meant the words figuratively and literally.

Valon didn't seem bothered. "I know you think I'm dodging you. I'm not. This job honestly is nonstop. If I ever sit still, someone better will take my place. There's no such thing as legends anymore. There's someone new around every corner, just one internet sound bite away from stealing my spot."

Ledger could see that. He already knew he was a passing internet fad. That was one reason he had fought so hard against hiring security. Give it six months. No one would remember him.

"Not everyone is you." Kash said the words with his gaze still locked on that goddamn menu. "You'll be a legend." There was no flattery in the statement. Kash sounded exactly as if he stated a known fact.

Valon's gaze moved Kash's way for the first time. Something akin to sadness passed over Valon's features. "You've always believed in me more than I believe in myself."

Kash never looked up, and the moment passed as quickly as it came. Then Valon was focused on Ledger again, and Ledger had never been more torn in two in his life. Throughout Valon's entire life,

Ledger had happily made every sacrifice for him. There had never been a choice to make. His son came first, full stop. This one time, Ledger wasn't sure what to do. Whatever was happening between Kash and him, Ledger didn't think he could quit it. He knew exactly how shitty that made him.

The day had taken a sharp turn at lunch. Kash wished he could leave, so Ledger could enjoy some time with his son. Except he was Ledger's bodyguard now, and he had no choice but to be subjected to more of Valon and how the world revolved around him. Always had. While he had once been happily inside that orbit, he wasn't that guy anymore. He was beyond fucking relieved when they made it home. Not only did Kash have a lot to put away, but his goddamn luggage sat on the front porch. Now he had extra baggage to lug around when he moved on, and he would move on. He was glad Valon pulled his head out of his ass and showed up for Ledger. But Kash saw Ledger's face at lunch. He was done with Kash.

Kash took the tags off his new clothes and grabbed the whole pile. The laundry room was on the opposite side of the house from where father and son caught up with each other. Kash smashed everything inside the washer. He didn't give a fuck if anything got ruined. Only the strong survived in his life. He picked a setting that seemed fair and threw in all the soapy, smell-good shit. It was like being at a laundromat. He had spent a lot of days as a kid sitting inside a rundown laundromat, watching clothes go around in a circle. He had gotten pretty good at entertaining himself for hours doing absolutely nothing. Who knew that practice in patience would help him later in life when stalking targets? While unpacking his bags, he found the only thing he cared about losing. His tiny sketchbook with the comic strip he had drawn. He had a new idea. He had shoved his pencils and notebook in his back pocket to keep him company while he waited. Kash settled on the floor. He scooted his large frame between two oversized hampers so he could lean against the wall. Using his bent knees as a writing surface, he flipped to the first blank page he found.

Kash turned inward and let the visions in his head pour onto the page. Occasionally, he caught himself chuckling at his character's antics. His character Dash was always the same, finding trouble everywhere he looked. Things always worked out in the end, though. Everyone deserved a happy ending. Before he knew it, the washer chimed, alerting him to the end of its cycle. Kash set his things aside and switched the clothes to the dryer before disappearing again. Time moved at lightning pace when he was in the zone. He saw three drawings ahead, and he couldn't get them on the page quickly enough. Kash knew he would have to go back later and fix the parts that looked rushed. Sometimes he wished he could just open his head and pour out his visions onto paper. He couldn't draw anywhere near as fast as he could think. The dryer chimed, and Kash didn't move. He was too engrossed to notice. When he lifted his head again, his neck popped. Kash blinked in surprise at the sight of his clothes neatly folded in a basket. He glanced around. No one was there.

Curiosity and a backache brought Kash to his feet. He gathered everything and headed for his room. The house was silent. As he neared his room, he spotted Ledger's open door. He slowed and peeked inside. The bedside lamp was on. Ledger slept peacefully with his glasses on and an open book resting on his chest. Kash dropped his stuff in his bedroom doorway and slipped inside Ledger's room. He moved in total silence. Kash set the book aside, open and face-down so Ledger wouldn't lose his page. With that out of the way, he carefully removed Ledger's glasses and set them beside the book. He took a moment to memorize Ledger's face before turning off the light. In his entire life, nothing had ever been meant to be his. This dream was no different. Ledger was a solid person. He would always only see Kash as his son's ex. Too young. Off limits. Kash went to his room and closed the door. He rubbed his chest. Tomorrow, Kash would call Steel and get a replacement. Kash had never been meant for good things. He had to stop pretending he could be anything else.

Chapter Six

After a night of drawing, Kash ran on two hours of sleep and annoyance. He had listened to Ledger toss and turn all night. Kash ended up giving up two hours ago. After a shower, he grabbed the first clothes he found and headed for the kitchen. After scavenging for a few minutes, he ended up making pancakes. Ledger padded into the room with dark circles under his eyes.

"Hey. It looks like you got about as much sleep as I did."

A small smile touched Ledger's lips. "What's new, right?" He moved to stand next to Kash. "This is a lot of food. It looks good, though. I'm up for the challenge."

Kash shrugged. He tried to keep things impersonal. "I figured between Valon's new guards and the three of us, we needed a lot."

"Valon left last night. He had to be at the airport by four this morning. It was easier for him to stay at a nearby hotel than try to fight traffic this morning."

Kash was slightly relieved. He kept his heart out of it. "Well, I guess this is a lot of food, then."

Ledger laughed. The sound ran down Kash's spine, making his skin feel tighter. He really needed to hit the nearest club and find someone to fuck. Maybe that would be the first thing he did once Steel sent a replacement.

"What would you like to do today?"

Kash shook off his thoughts. "Just do what you usually do. I'm your guard. Not your guest. You don't have to entertain me."

"What if I want to entertain you?" The heat in Ledger's every word hurt way more than he liked. Kash remembered too many things now. The way he had felt when he had left town had been polished off and shone bright for Kash's inspection. He couldn't keep doing this to himself.

"After breakfast, I'll call Steel and have a replacement sent over."

Silence hung heavily between them.

Kash refused to look at Ledger.

Ledger spoke. His voice was quiet and had Kash meeting his gaze. "I wish you wouldn't do that."

Kash cocked his head to one side and studied Ledger. He looked genuinely hurt at the idea of Kash leaving. "What do you normally do during the week?"

A guarded but hopeful smile touched Ledger's lips. "I'm boring. You should show me what you're working on."

Everything inside Kash recoiled. His comic strips were personal. Something just for him. He couldn't crack himself open like that. Everyone had already stripped him of everything else. Kash couldn't taint this.

Kash poured syrup over his pancakes. "It's just doodling."

Ledger set his hand on Kash's forearm, holding his attention. "I watched you for a while last night. It's not just scribblings. You were too focused to even notice me. It was fascinating to watch. Your every emotion moved across your face. I'm a huge reader and nosy. I'd love to see what you saw."

Kash swallowed. Ledger looked serious. "Okay. Eat first." Fuck his entire life. What had he just agreed to do? He suddenly wasn't very hungry. Kash sat and put food in his mouth. It tasted like cardboard. All he could picture was Ledger laughing at him, or worse, humoring him.

Somehow, breakfast was gone, and it was like facing his reckoning. He tried to wash dishes to buy time.

Ledger hip-bumped him aside. “You cooked. I’ll clean. Go get your notepad.”

Kash felt like a kid being sent to his room to retrieve something he knew would get him in trouble. He didn’t grab the one from last night. That one wasn’t finished. If he was about to be humiliated, at least it could be over the best he could do. By the time he finished deciding which one, Ledger already waited for him in the living room.

Kash’s anxiety got the best of him. There were very few things Kash didn’t have top-tier confidence about. To the point of cockiness, really. But his art was his and only his, and this was a nightmare scenario for him. Kash hesitated as he handed the pad to Ledger.

“Don’t laugh at me.”

Ledger looked hurt over the insinuation. “This is part of you. I could never laugh at that.”

With a sharp nod, Kash let go of the notebook. He filled the spot next to Ledger on the couch. With his feet braced on the edge of the coffee table, he shoved his hands between his knees and took slow breaths.

Ledger silently flipped through the pages. He chuckled.

Kash’s gaze shot his way. He had no qualms about ripping the pad out of his hands.

Ledger was smiling as he read. His gaze moved over each page. Obviously, feeling his accusing stare, Ledger glanced his way. "I'm sorry. I'm not laughing at you. The story is hilarious. I love the way Dash uses a combination of flirting and over-the-top antics to brazen through." He dropped his hands to his lap, still holding the homemade comic. "This is amazing, Kash. You know I'm a book lover. This should be in every bookstore. You blow me away. How long have you been hiding this talent?"

Kash still wasn't sure if Ledger was only humoring him. He fought the urge to chew his nails. Kash shrugged. "Since I was a kid. I've spent a lot of time alone with nothing but my imagination. It's not like I had video games or even the internet like other kids, but these small spiral pads were easy to steal from the bookshop at school. I have a storage building where I keep them. There're a ton of them." Kash shrugged again. He felt exposed as hell. "It's not like I have a home or anything to keep them in, but I can't bring myself to throw them away."

With his head resting on the back of the couch, Ledger stared at him.

Kash fought the urge to squirm under Ledger's inspection. "I guess I should get rid of them. It seems crazy to cling to something so dumb."

"Nothing about you is dumb. You've just spent your entire life carrying everyone else on your shoulders." Ledger squeezed Kash's knee. "You're the best person I've ever had the pleasure of knowing.

There's still time for life to give you what you deserve."

He hated this conversation. Kash was uncomfortable. "Nah. I'm good. I've always known I won't live to be old. Honestly, I'm surprised I've made it this close to thirty." His knee bounced, proving how ready he was to run.

"Let the storage building go. Move everything here. Even if you don't decide to stay, this is your home now. I proclaim it so!" Ledger shouted. The words were filled with laughter.

Kash didn't laugh. He scratched the bridge of his nose. "I can't put you in that position. You're Valon's dad." Kash knew he should stop, but he didn't. He stared at the spot where the corner met the ceiling. Kash had no idea why he couldn't look at Ledger. "I saw the way your entire demeanor changed at lunch yesterday. You don't want me here. You'll always choose your son, as you should," Kash added before Ledger thought he would ever expect anything different. "I can't watch you hate me because I am who I am and you are who you are. That's one thing I can't live with. I've already had to lose you once."

"Valon told me you lectured him after I walked away yesterday. Believe it or not, yours is the only opinion that's ever mattered to him. He says everyone else is fake, except you. You don't give a fuck about how anyone feels about you, and that makes you more honest than anyone else. I know there's nothing left between you two, but he still respects your thoughts. So do I, but on this topic, you're wrong."

Kash couldn't stop his eyes from turning Ledger's way.

Ledger boldly held his stare. "I want you here."

"Okay." His soft agreement surprised him more than anyone. He hadn't even thought. His mouth had simply decided. Kash didn't know how to tell Ledger no.

Ledger stood. "Good. Let's go get your things out of storage."

Kash laughed. "What makes you think my storage unit is here?"

Ledger's eyebrows rose. "Educated guess."

Kash shook his head and stood. “It’s an hour drive. If we get started now, we can be back in time for me to take you out for the day.”

Ledger’s eyes glowed with happiness. “Won’t we technically be out already?”

“We’ll see if you feel the same later.”

Ledger shook his head, but his sexy smile was every bit as happy-looking as Kash’s felt. Kash refused to lose hope yet. As long as Ledger looked at him the way he did now, Kash feared he would never give up.

Until Ledger saw the inside of Kash's storage unit, he hadn't thought his heart could break for him any more than it already had. For half a second, Ledger's gaze landed on the old beat-up car inside, and nostalgia washed over him. Kash had been seventeen when he came into their lives. On the first day of freshman year, Valon had come home via this piece of metal. Ledger had no idea how Kash kept it running. Valon had introduced Kash to Ledger. Of course, Ledger had grilled him. Kash was two years older than Valon with more freedom, a car, and he looked exactly like he would have Valon on drugs within a month. Instead, Ledger met a funny guy with high intelligence who lifted Valon up to be greater than he ever could be alone. All Kash had needed was a chance. His only sin was being poor with an alcoholic mother. That wasn't his fault. He had no control over his circumstances. Ledger had quickly learned Kash got up at four a.m. every day to work for a local mechanic. Then he went to school and bagged groceries at night. The mechanic had made sure the car was in good running condition and gave it to Kash so he could make it to work. Kash had bills to pay at home. He didn't have time to get into trouble. Yet he always made time for them. Seeing that car again brought back way too many memories. Then Ledger's gaze skimmed the rest of the room and emotions clogged his throat. A few plastic storage totes were in the corner, holding Kash's art. There was one metal shelf. All it had on it was Kash's mom's ashes, and every birthday and Christmas gift Ledger had ever given him.

"I can donate the car to charity, so it's not hogging a spot in your garage needlessly. I don't know why I've hung on to it."

Ledger shook his head. He had to swallow past a lump in his throat to speak. "If you want to keep it, I have room for it... unless you own three more cars I don't know about." Ledger infused as much humor as he could into the statement.

Kash didn't laugh or look his way. "Yeah, I do, but they're all in various storage units around the country." Kash popped the trunk of the car and pulled out two duffel bags. He carried them to Ledger's Navigator and stuffed them in the backseat.

All Ledger could do was watch while he processed Kash's claim. After a moment, he blew out a sigh. "I'll get the boxes from the SUV." He circled the vehicle and opened the back. Kash had said they would need a couple of boxes to pack everything. He had truly meant a couple of small boxes.

Ledger carefully packed Kash's mom's ashes first, making sure they wouldn't move around too much. The sight of the box that held the ashes along with him actually holding it gave Ledger a much-needed reality check. This was still the temporary container given to Kash by the funeral home. Ledger should have forced Kash to accept his help, even if only to buy a proper urn.

Ledger chanced to mention it while Kash packed away the gifts. "We should get her a proper urn, don't you think?"

"That was my plan. But I haven't been back to California in a long time. I haven't gotten a chance to deal with it."

Ledger pushed a little more. "I can get it for you if you'd like. Since I've lost a lot of family, I'm way too familiar with picking them."

"If you want the job, it's yours. Just use my debit card to get whatever. You didn't know her any better than I did."

He couldn't take it. Ledger stood. He held Kash's stare, so Kash knew he meant every word he said. "You deserved better." He motioned around the room. "You deserved a hell of a lot more than this small shelf of memories. I'm furious with myself for not doing more."

Kash didn't look upset by the borderline-yelled words. "It wasn't your place to do more. I was five months away from eighteen when we met. All you could've done was have me spending five months in foster care, and that would've been worse. She died four months later anyhow. I was damn near already the adult I've always had to be when we met. You couldn't change things any more than I could. Don't torture yourself with the past." Kash's entire demeanor turned more intense by the second. "You're looking at the man I am now. Don't ever think of me as a weak kid again."

Ledger was transfixed. Tension built between them. "I've never seen you as a kid, much less weak."

Kash took a step closer. "How do you see me?"

It got a little harder to breathe. There was nowhere to run. "Please don't make me answer that."

Kash shook his head. "You don't have to say it."

Ledger's breathing turned rapid. He saw life through a pinpoint. Kash stared at him a way Ledger had tried to forget. Ledger hadn't realized exactly how close Kash had gotten until Kash's lips touched his. He couldn't scramble away with the car so closely behind him. In fact, he was pressed against the vehicle with no clue how he had gotten there. He couldn't lie to himself and say he hadn't seen the kiss coming. Ledger knew exactly why he had gotten so lost in Kash's blue eyes. He wanted this. Ledger hated how weak he was, but then again, he didn't. Kash had Ledger in knots. He didn't know if he wanted him to stop.

Kash held Ledger's bottom lip between his and didn't move. Ledger knew he waited for Ledger to decide the next move. His heart beat so loudly, there was no way Kash didn't hear it. Even to his ears, Ledger sounded on the edge of hyperventilating. Ledger's thoughts were all over the place. Right now, he could stop and call it an innocent kiss. If his lips parted, everything would change. He would have to admit he wanted his son's ex. Ledger didn't know if he could cross that line. He needed Kash to choose and take the burden from him.

"Kash Humphries?"

Kash backed away and went on high alert.

His body language had Ledger spinning to see who interrupted them. A man in expensive-looking black dress pants and a perfectly pressed white button-down stood in the mouth of the storage unit. Only one detail stood out above the rest. He had a badge clipped to his belt.

"Depends on who's asking." Kash's voice sounded different—harder.

"Detective Smith Avery. I just need to ask a few questions."

Kash became someone else. His eyes swam with malicious mirth. An evil-looking smile stretched his lips. “Not without my lawyer you don’t, and why do you have a first name that should be your last and a last name that should be your first?”

Ledger couldn’t say why. It was hella bad timing, but a laugh burst from him. The spiel had been delivered with such wry humor; he couldn’t stop the sound.

Smith’s eyes swam with laughter as Ledger covered his mouth. God, Ledger had no idea why this man, standing inches from him, made him feel so much like he was the younger one and Kash was in charge.

The detective looked between them before focusing on Kash again. “You don’t need your attorney for this. The general just needs a few answers."

Ledger was super confused by the claim.

Kash's entire attitude shifted. He took a step toward Smith.

Ledger stopped him. "Don't let them trick you into talking to them without a lawyer. They always say you don't need one, and you do."

Kash kissed his cheek. "I promise I'm good." He walked away, leaving Ledger floundering. The general of what had questions? That was a seriously odd assertion. Did Kash do some sort of work for the government?

Ledger being Ledger, protecting his boy, circled the car to listen while staying out of sight.

"You haven't responded to any texts from the general in a few days."

"I told Ajax where I am. See how easily you were able to find me. If he needs any jobs done on the west coast, then we're solid. As of right now, I have no plans to return to Atlantic City. He knows this. Everything I love is here."

Ledger stopped breathing.

"Call him. I'm just the messenger."

Kash sounded calm and honest. He didn't sound as if there was anything to worry about. "Tell him I'll call him tonight. I'm not dodging him. We're good."

"I'll let him know." The detective sounded as if he believed.

Ledger didn't know if he should be worried. While the entire conversation didn't feel malevolent in any way, Kash had admitted to shady dealings. But this was a cop, and he didn't sound like Kash had done anything wrong other than not answering some general.

The sound of a car door closing pulled him from his musings. An engine started. Ledger didn't move from his spot. He wanted honesty between them. Whatever was happening between them would already turn Ledger's life upside down. If he risked everything on lies, Ledger couldn't handle that. He already didn't know what he was doing.

Kash stepped back inside. His gaze went straight to Ledger like he had never lost sight of him.

Ledger didn't wait for the other shoe to drop. He threw it. "Who's Ajax?"

Kash moved his way. Ledger was almost distracted by the way his body held so much confidence—the way he moved like a predator. "General Ajax is head of the Royal Guard for Prince Noir Antonsen of the Republic of Serveno. That's who I work for."

"Oh." Ledger knew he sounded as clueless as he was.

Kash sat on the hood of the car and held Ledger's stare. "Noir lives in the U.S. as a diplomat for his country. He was sent here to be a symbol of trust, unity, and alliance with the United States. Since Noir is too far down in the line of succession to ever be king, his life is here." Kash hesitated.

Ledger pressed. "You can always talk to me."

Kash's mouth lifted in one corner. "I know. That's the problem. I can tell you anything. Sometimes not knowing is what keeps you safe."

Ledger growled. He couldn't stop the sound. "I don't like you being cryptic. You act like you intend to stay here and be a part of my life. If you're doing something that I could go to prison for, ignorant of those doings or not, I'd prefer to know. For fuck's sake, I haven't called the cops or told you to hit the road yet. I don't want to be with someone who keeps secrets. Secrets ruined my whole goddamn life. You were there for it. I would rather spend the rest of my life never hearing from or seeing anyone else than fall in love with someone who lies."

Ledger was so angry, he didn't even know what he said anymore, nor did he care.

Since the moment he saw Kash again, everything he had suppressed and hidden away came rushing back and everything was choking him—the same as it had done back then. He had survived a terrible marriage, losing his son to fame, and watching this man—who had been his best friend, sad as that might be—vanish into the night without a word or goodbye. Ledger didn't want to go through any more heartbreak. He was tired. "You already—"

Ledger scrubbed his hands through his hair. His frustration was frustrated. He wasn't supposed to feel anything for Kash. It was wrong on so many levels. He didn't want this, but he did, and what did that say about him? Ledger headed for the truck. Kash could use all the secrets he had to find a way home. Ledger couldn't do this.

He didn't make it three steps before he found his back shoved against the wall.

Kash didn't look angry. He looked downright terrifying. "Say it."

Ledger couldn't breathe. The harder he sucked air into his lungs, the less oxygen he got.

Kash didn't let up. He shuffled closer, boxing Ledger in even tighter, creating a bubble only they existed in. "Say it, Ledger. Finish that thought. If you can't say it to me, then you're the one with secrets. I left to save you from this. Don't lie to yourself or me and say you didn't know it. So tell me now or set me free."

Ledger realized he clung tightly to Kash's shirt. Two handfuls of the material were in his grasp like he couldn't decide if he wanted to pull Kash closer or shove him away.

Kash managed to move an inch closer.

Ledger's body begged to have Kash pressed against it. "You already left once, and you're supposed to be mine." He didn't get a chance to regret anything. Kash's mouth covered his. He was everywhere. They were the same size, and still somehow Kash made Ledger feel like he would always protect him. The way Kash kissed him had Ledger's entire body lit. His kiss was all-consuming. He licked and sucked while Ledger hung on for the ride. Their bodies just fit together.

Kash's kiss slowed and softened.

Ledger's eyes burned from the sweetness of it. There was no right or wrong in Kash's arms. They simply existed for each other for a moment sliced from time. Tears rolled down Ledger's cheeks. It took him a second to realize they weren't his.

Ledger jerked his head backward.

Kash swiped his cheeks before resting his forehead against Ledger's. "I gave up."

Without thinking, Ledger's hands found their way beneath Kash's t-shirt. He had to touch bare skin. He needed the heat and flesh between his hands so he knew this wasn't a dream. "I'm here."

Kash reclaimed Ledger's mouth in a sweet kiss. Their lips lingered, clinging. He felt the shift between them like a physical thing. This was happening. There was no going back.

Chapter Seven

The first free moment Kash had, he called Ajax. While he had lived in Atlantic City, he had made the mistake of doing collections and making drops for the biggest drug lord on the east coast. Noir ran Atlantic City with an iron fist. Not to mention, the guy was certifiably insane. He didn't send anyone to do his dirty work if he wanted someone dead. It was rumored he had once stabbed a man to death, leaving behind enough holes to make anyone else drop in exhaustion. People said the coroner gave up trying to count them. Noir wasn't one to be fucked with. Ajax guarded a psychopath. What did that say about what he was capable of doing? The absolute dumbest thing he had done was leave Atlantic City as if he planned to return. He hadn't covered his tracks and led this entire mess straight to Ledger's door. The only defense he had was that he hadn't expected to see Ledger and have every feeling rush back to him like he had been kept in stasis since they last saw each other. Kash hadn't experienced more than lust for anyone since walking away from this town. There was no way he could've known there was a reason for that. It turned out Ledger had been more than a temporary, secret obsession; he had stolen Kash. He couldn't see anyone else.

Kash sat on hold for longer than necessary. He knew Ajax did it on purpose. Kash had once flirted with the man Ajax had been head over heels in love with for years. He had not made any friends in that one.

"You've been dodging me."

No hi or checking to see if Kash was actually on the line. "I'm sorry you see it that way. I spoke with Noir before leaving town. You two know where I am. That's not dodging. My life just doesn't revolve around you." It was a calculated risk, feeding Ajax attitude, but he wouldn't let Ajax think he was some weak-ass bitch he could push around.

A moment of silence lingered. Someone spoke in the background. Ajax released a loud, put-upon sigh. “You’re lucky my man likes you.”

He was lucky he had dirt on Ajax’s man. Kash was the only person who knew he had given Lucas an out card, in case he ever needed to leave Ajax.

“I like him too.” Kash ensured he poured as much sexual promise into the words as possible.

Ledger glanced up from cooking with raised eyebrows.

Kash winked.

Another loud sigh brushed his ear. “Yeah. I think I like you better on the opposite coast. I don’t put it past you to keep trying your luck until I’m forced to kill you.”

A smile exploded across Kash's face. He might not have much going for him, but Kash knew how to drive people in the direction they needed to go.

"I'll inform Noir this move is a permanent one. Do not lose touch with me again. Same rules apply. Do your job. We'll keep you safe. Everyone makes money. Don't make a liar out of me, Kash. This move is permanent, even if I have to come there to kill you. Understood?"

"I'm not worried. You know I'm a good boy."

Ledger smiled and shook his head.

Ajax snorted and disconnected the call. With a chuckle, Kash tossed the phone aside. There. Ledger protected. He still had a source of money and the prince's protection. More than anything, he had

Ledger all alone. To himself. Bonus points, Ledger wanted him too. Kash didn't know how much patience he had in him tonight. They had moved Kash's things in, along with his car. Kash had canceled his storage unit. It had been a full day. Now they were home. Truthfully, it still didn't feel like home. He was still braced for this to fall apart before things even got started. After all, Valon always won. The moment he caught wind of this, Ledger would be done.

Right now, though, Kash could do this. He moved to stand behind Ledger and molded against his back. He buried his nose against Ledger's neck. "Mhmm. Something smells good. I'm excited to taste it."

He felt more than heard Ledger chuckle. "I hope you're not disappointed with your decision. With everything going on, I haven't hit the gym in the last few days. I'm already turning into flab."

Kash gave Ledger his space. "I'm not worried. You make me way too hot. But you should let me know your usual gym schedule. I've been lax too. While you're at it, I need your typical schedule for every day of the week, so I can set up a solid security plan. We've been winging it, and that's not smart. If someone's determined to get to you, they'll follow your normal path. Everyone has a daily pattern, whether they mean to or not. It's all well and good to say mix it up and keep them guessing. But that's not realistic if you want a settled life, and I want a settled life."

The sweet smile that touched Ledger's lips made Kash's heart beat a little faster.

"Do you practice these lines in the mirror?"

That one confused Kash. "What do you mean?"

For a moment, Ledger just stared at him. Then he shook his head. "Wow. You really mean it. You're ready to jump into life with me with both feet. No overthinking or regrets."

It seemed Ledger still didn't fully understand how serious Kash was. Kash knew himself. Not only did he want to dive right in, Kash might do anything if anyone thwarted his plans. He had waited a long time to have Ledger without all the guilt and ugly bits. He didn't know how long they had before they had to face the firing squad named Valon, but he needed to savor every second. Cooking was taking too long.

"No overthinking. No regrets. Just us."

A slight blush touched Ledger's cheeks, fascinating Kash. "What's this about? Why are you blushing?"

Ledger looked away and focused on stirring pots. After a moment, he cleared his throat and met Kash's stare. "I haven't been with anyone since Ry left."

Kash didn't react. He wasn't the least bit surprised. Ledger was loyal and believed in love. He wouldn't jump from bed to bed. Ledger needed something real. He had found it. "I can go slow." In fact, he looked forward to savoring every second of a body he never thought he would have. The heart attached was the sexiest part, but Kash would be lying if he said it wasn't also about sex. He very much wanted Ledger every way he could have him.

"That was a lot of flirting on the phone. What did you learn?"

"Ah. The deflection." He would let it stand. Kash understood Ry's betrayal would linger with them for a while until Kash proved he would never do the same. "There're only two things Ajax loves: his prince and his man, Lucas, and Ajax is a jealous bastard. The best way to stay on this coast is for Ajax to want me as far away from Lucas as possible." Kash spread his arms wide. "Here I am, ordered to stay right where I am for good."

Ledger looked skeptical. "And they want nothing in return?"

Kash needed Ledger to know he would always be honest. “I definitely didn’t say that. People don’t walk away from crime lords and live to talk. Not to mention, there isn’t a single law or government agency that isn’t bought and paid for. I’m sorry I brought this to your door. When I got here, I expected you to take one look at me and tell me to leave. If I had thought there was a single hope you might love me someday, I would’ve covered my every step. You know I can vanish when I want to. I never thought someone like you would ever touch someone like me.”

“Don’t say shit like that.” Ledger looked fierce. “Stop acting like I’m some prize who isn’t more than twenty years older than you. I’m not Ajax. You don’t have to corner me with compliments or apologize for a bad decision when you never thought you'd be here again. Granted, being tied to a crime lord is pretty fucking massive." Ledger made a gesture like wiping away his words. "That's not the point right now." He took a deep breath, as if calming himself. Ledger held his stare. "I know I'm a lot older than you. Maybe I look good right now, but I won't forever, so I fully understand you'll eventually want someone else. But I absolutely want as much of you as I can get until you move on."

Kash let Ledger unload that bullshit, so he didn't have to carry it, but goddamn. For a moment, he simply blinked while trying to decide how he felt. "Well, that was the dumbest thing I've ever heard." Kash couldn't deny the anger growing inside him. "No. I'm actually furious. I've spent years incapable of anything serious with anyone else because you've been lodged in my head." Kash pushed all the buttons to turn off the cooktop built into the island. "It pisses me the fuck off that you could think I'm anything like Ry, but I get it. He was a terrible person impersonating a good husband." Kash met and held Ledger's gaze. "I'm someone who has been sickeningly in love with you for years, while disguised as a bad guy. If you want to eat any of this tonight, then stop toying with me. I'll absolutely spank you until you learn your lesson."

Ledger visibly fought not to smile. "What lesson is that?"

Kash snagged Ledger's hips and towed Ledger against him. He wanted Ledger to feel how hard he was for him. "That you're mine and I'm no fucking cheat.

You're sexy as fuck, always have been, but this isn't about looks. It's you. Everything about you makes me hot as hell, especially your sexy heart." Kash followed the waistband of Ledger's jeans to the front and then popped the button. His gaze never wavered from Ledger's eyes. "I already know I'll never get sick of touching you." He slowly slid Ledger's zipper down as he watched a flush grow across Ledger's cheeks. Yeah, he wanted this too. "That's what it's like being an addict. Even if you find a way to get sober, for the rest of your life, that craving stays in the back of your mind, lurking. You're the only addiction I have, and I don't want to get clean." He shoved his hand inside Ledger's underwear. Pre-cum smeared his skin as he slid his hand down the length of Ledger's erection, torturing them both. "I want to get very, very dirty."

Ledger licked his lips, looking slightly nervous but incredibly aroused. "Okay."

Damn. Kash really was addicted. He never wanted to stop.

Holy shit. That really was all Ledger could think. Twenty years of being married to someone who lied, kept secrets, and never wanted to talk things through made Kash seem too good to be true. He communicated. Kash didn't let things fester. Whatever he felt, he said it. If Ledger felt insecure or worried in any way, Kash wiped the negativity away. Maybe one day he would find out the hard way none of this was real. Until then, Ledger craved everything Kash's eyes promised.

Kash kissed him, twirling his tongue in Ledger's mouth while he slowly stroked Ledger's cock. His mouth moved to Ledger's ear. "Tell me how you want it. There's nothing I won't do."

Whoa. The nervousness slipped away. Kash was too intense for Ledger to feel anything except horny. Plus, Kash wasn't looking at him. He was busy kissing Ledger's throat.

"I'm a switch. I like it all."

"Good answer." Kash dropped to his knees.

Ledger's first thought was about Kash's knees. They had to hurt on this hard floor. Then his dick was in Kash's mouth, and Ledger stopped thinking. He hadn't lied about it being a long time since anyone had touched him. Not only had he been divorced for years, but Ry had also stopped touching him long before that. That should have been his first clue about the affairs. Ledger had been too busy trying to be whatever Ry needed, so he let go of his needs. They roared back now.

Ledger's fingers dove into Kash's dark blond hair. He held on as he rolled his hips, taking what he wanted. Ledger knew it was Kash on his dick. Between that and how fucking good Kash's mouth felt, Ledger wouldn't make it long. Right before he could blow and embarrass himself, Kash shot to his feet. He held Ledger's hand, dragging him toward the bedroom.

"When you come, it'll be sitting on my dick. I'm not missing that."

Ledger could barely breathe. Kash had him half out of his mind with need.

When Kash reached the bed, he spun, lifted Ledger off his feet, and tossed him onto the bed.

Ledger's lust tripled at the show of strength.

Kash hovered over him. "You said it's been a long time. Do you have any of the things we need?"

"Lube."

"I'll be right back. When I get back, you'd better be nude."

Without waiting for Ledger to argue, not that he would, Kash headed for the door. The moment he was out of sight, Ledger scrambled out of his clothes. He didn't know what Kash's punishment would be if Ledger disobeyed. But if Kash withheld sex to teach him a lesson, Ledger might literally die. It already took everything he possessed not to reach down and finish himself. He was a desperate man.

Kash returned totally nude. He ripped open a condom with his teeth as he headed Ledger's way. His features were so harsh, Ledger wondered if he should be scared. Then Kash crawled onto the bed. He kissed Ledger while simultaneously rolling on the condom.

Ledger smacked the bedside table, searching for the knob on the drawer so he could get the lube. His book and glass-es hit the floor.

Kash's mouth tore away. His gaze shot toward the struggling. "You're all good. I came prepared. I've got you." Wet fingers toyed with his asshole.

Ledger forgot his own name. Kash had him twisted in lust to the point of not even seeing Kash carry lube into the room. He was older. Ledger should be the one reassuring Kash. But Ledger had a feeling Kash was about to rock him hard enough Ledger would never think of him as younger again.

“Look at me.”

Ledger immediately obeyed Kash’s demanding tone. His gaze shot straight to holding Kash’s stare.

Kash never broke eye contact as he inched his way in, stopping several times for Ledger to adjust. It took Ledger a moment to realize Kash watched for any signs of pain in Ledger’s eyes. He had never felt as seen as he did right then. Ledger felt like Kash stared into his soul.

“What do you see?” The whispered words wouldn’t be stopped.

Kash’s expression never lost an ounce of intensity. “Everything.”

His body gave way.

Kash gently pumped inside him. He shifted his angle and Ledger's position until he obviously found what he wanted in Ledger's reactions. Then everything fell away.

Kash grabbed the headboard and used the leverage to take what he wanted. Every breath Ledger took matched Kash's rhythm. Ledger wanted to move and take more of what he needed, but Kash had him as twisted as a pretzel. The connection was fierce. All the years of pretending and shameful desire collided into a single act. Ledger more than knew nothing would ever be the same. It already wasn't. He would never look at Kash again without envisioning this. They were headed somewhere together.

The slow, calculated thrusts got harder and faster. Ledger scratched at the sheets and Kash's skin. The need for release crushed him. Pretty soon, his heart would stop if he didn't blow.

"You're beautiful clinging to the edge. I could keep you here all night."

Ledger strained.

A sexy moan rumbled from Kash. "That's it. Use me. It's just us. Take what you need."

Ledger's impatience beat him. Using every ounce of his strength, Ledger flipped, taking Kash to the mattress. With Kash trapped beneath him, Ledger rode him hard while nipping at Kash's chest. He had to taste the sexy, hard, tattooed masterpiece trapped under him. Ledger couldn't think. Pure lust drove his every move. Kash cried out.

Ledger barely heard him. His ears popped and rang as the most powerful orgasm he had ever experienced took away his ability to function. He kept riding Kash until there wasn't a single twitch of pleasure left. Before he could collapse and recover, Kash grabbed his jaw and torched his mouth in the hungriest of kisses. There was no coming down when Kash was involved.

The kiss softened, turning loving. Their fingers linked. It was as if they fought to hang on to any connection.

"I don't want to stop." Kash's whispered confession between kisses nearly broke him. He sounded like he was empty and lost without Ledger's touch. Kash wasn't alone. The way Ledger felt scared the shit out of him. He felt a hell of a lot like he would do anything to keep this. Even at the cost of his son.

Chapter Eight

It wasn't hard to keep Ledger safe. The first few weeks of never leaving the house, Kash hadn't really noticed. They got their full workout every day using Ledger's home gym. Kash couldn't keep his hands off Ledger, so he had no interest in being anywhere else. It wasn't until Kash really looked at things that he realized Ledger never did much of anything other than read, make videos and block disgusting people online. He had always known Ledger to be an outgoing, active guy. They used to do a lot of fun shit together. Kash wasn't complaining. If all he ever did again was enjoy Ledger's company and body, he would die a happy man. Kash wasn't worried about himself. He couldn't imagine this existence making Ledger happy in the long run.

Kash paused in the middle of working on a sketch. He glanced Ledger's way. Ledger looked engrossed in his book. Kash considered leaving the subject alone, but he couldn't.

"I'm surprised you don't want to go shopping or to the library or something."

Ledger glanced over in surprise. "Oh. I haven't really gone out much since the threats started about eight months ago. Things ramped up pretty hard shortly before you got here. I started finding gifts on my car everywhere I went and notes taped to the front door. It's one thing for people to say shit online. It's a whole other when you feel like people are watching you every second of the day."

That irritated Kash more than just a little. "Why didn't you say anything when I got here? I can keep you safe anywhere you want to go, but it's helpful for you to tell me *everything* you've been going through." He didn't mean to sound so accusatory, but fuck. People were physically stalking him to the point of leaving shit on his car. That was need-to-know information.

Ledger shrugged. "Like I said, I don't really go anywhere anymore, so I didn't think about it."

Kash stood and set his sketch on the coffee table before taking Ledger's book and setting it next to the sketch. He lured Ledger to his feet. "We're not doing this hiding shit. You're not giving up your life over a few insane people. We're going to the boardwalk and hitting the food trucks."

Ledger chuckled as he let himself get dragged along. "Food poisoning be damned, eh?"

Kash couldn't stop smiling. He didn't give Ledger a chance to say no. Kash had his shoes on, waiting on Ledger to put his on too in under a minute.

Ledger wore a luminous smile and kept shaking his head as if Kash drove him crazy.

Kash had to look away to keep from jumping him. Ledger was under his skin in every way. He never got enough. The moment they were ready, he headed into the garage and straight to Ledger's SUV. They climbed inside and buckled their seatbelts. Kash looked Ledger's way to make sure he was good. He found Ledger turned sideways with his head resting against the headrest, staring.

A smile exploded across Kash's face. "What?"

"Nothing. I'm just admiring the view."

Ledger really kept him smiling like an idiot. "I'm trying to get *out* of the house. Not in bed."

Ledger laughed and sat properly.

Kash shook his head and hit the button to open the garage. He slowly backed out and made sure the door closed firmly behind him before clicking the button on the key fob to set the alarm. Once they were on their way, Kash automatically reached for Ledger's hand. When Ledger linked fingers with him, it hit Kash. He had truly grown accustomed to being one half of a pair. Without thinking, he always touched Ledger or shifted closer. The moment Ledger had agreed to keep him, Kash had jumped straight into the role of a lifetime. Holding hands was such a small thing. Kash couldn't live without this again.

Thanks to traffic, it took nearly half an hour to reach their destination. Another ten minutes to find a place to park and five minutes to walk the distance after they finally found something. The scent of competing food smells wafted around them. There was a long line for tacos while a few people watched candy bars being deep fried. Another cart spun cotton candy. Kash forgot for a moment to check the crowd for anyone looking a little too hard in Ledger's direction.

"I haven't been here in years."

Kash focused on Ledger at the statement. "Me either. I used to hitchhike here when I was a kid. I'd walk by, smelling every stand, wishing I could afford anything at all. Truthfully, every time I left, I couldn't decide whether I felt better or worse. I got to enjoy all the colors, sounds, and smells, but I also was reminded of how different and poor I was."

"It kills me how many stories you have like that."

Kash's gaze skimmed the crowd. "It's all good. I can get whatever I want now."

Ledger's fingertips skimmed Kash's arm, pulling his attention Ledger's way. "Tell me what you always wished for the hardest while you were here. All I ever did was lose way too many quarters in those machines that push out more quarters and prizes over the edge if you do it just right, except they're rigged of course. So let's focus on you."

Kash chuckled while keeping his eyes moving. Being out in the open like this was a challenge, but Kash was up for anything if Ledger was happy. "I know the machines you mean. When I walked past them, I would always feel around and see if anyone had left any quarters in the tray. Once I found two, and when I played them, I won a cigarette lighter."

A loud, surprised-sounding laugh burst from Ledger. "You would've been better off keeping the coins."

Kash realized he was smiling. "Nah. I made a lot of campfires with that lighter. That mattered a lot when Mom would bring home strange men, and I stayed away to keep safe."

"You said that wearing a smile. Meanwhile, I'm thinking of getting your mom an urn with *Burn in Hell* engraved on it."

Kash couldn't help but laugh at Ledger's outrage.

"Those were some of my best memories. I was free and under the stars. Just me and my notebooks and dreams of running away. It was probably the most peace I got back then."

Ledger didn't respond.

Kash realized Ledger was more pissed off than he wanted to show. Kash shifted slightly, moving closer. "The fried cream cookies with whipped cream and chocolate syrup on top. That's what I always wished I could get."

"Then that's what we'll do first." Ledger pushed in that direction, dodging the crowd like a man on a mission.

Love swelled in Kash's chest. Ledger was the only person Kash had truly shared his past with. Throughout childhood, he had feared anyone knowing what his home life was like because foster care was a hell of a lot worse. So he stayed quiet. Something about Ledger always made him crack himself open for inspection.

Kash watched Ledger's back while he ordered. He kept one ear on the conversation so he could pay. Ledger was too quick for him. He swiped his card so fast, Kash couldn't even get out his wallet.

"I'll pay you back tonight."

The look Ledger shot him would've frozen boiling water in an instant. "Don't cheapen this moment."

Kash laughed at the bossy tone. He really was in love.

The guy in the booth handed Ledger two paper bowls that looked like diabetes. They ate as they walked. Silently, they eyed the sights. Neither of them spoke for several minutes.

Ledger shoved a bite into his mouth. He spoke around the food. "You know, this is actually pretty fucking disgusting."

Kash burst out laughing. "It really is, isn't it?"

In unison, they turned toward the nearest trash can.

Kash had a thought. He stopped Ledger before he could throw his bowl away. "Wait. I'm never doing this again, so we need a trophy." He pulled out his phone and opened the camera. "Come here." They put their heads together. Ledger held up his bowl between them. They both laughed, and Kash snapped their picture.

He couldn't stop smiling at the image.

Ledger took his bowl and threw them both away before sliding in close to check out the picture. "That turned out surprisingly good."

Kash nodded. "We look happy." He saved the image as his wallpaper on his phone. When he looked over, he found Ledger staring at him in a way he couldn't decipher. "What?" Even Kash heard the nervous laughter in his voice. Ledger looked entirely too intense.

"Ledger?"

Kash went on full alert at the sound of Ledger's name, forgetting all about the strange moment. He made himself look bigger, attempting to protect Ledger from every angle. If Ledger was about to get mobbed, Kash would keep him safe.

Ledger turned. His expression snapped completely closed. "Ry."

Kash was stunned into forgetting his job. If Ledger hadn't said his name, Kash never would've recognized him. Not only had Ry already been considerably older than Ledger, but the years had not been kind. He looked as if he had spent every minute of his life in a tanning booth while simultaneously getting bad plastic surgery to stretch out the wrinkles on his face. Kash had never experienced such a gut wrench desire to punch someone first and ask questions later.

Ry looked a little too excited to see Ledger. "Hey. How have you been?"

Ledger subtly shifted Kash's way, telling Kash everything he needed to know about this encounter. "I've been great. How about you?"

Kash wasn't one to act and play nice just because that was what society expected. His every molecule screamed they should just walk away.

Ry's gaze flickered Kash's way for half a second before dismissing him. "I'm good. I actually saw you two about three weeks ago, but I was too far away to say hi. Obviously, I was a bit surprised to see you two together. I called Valon to see if they had gotten back together. He says Kash is your bodyguard now?"

Kash nearly laughed. Ry couldn't try any harder to pretend Kash wasn't standing there.

"My son is famous. He worries."

It got harder by the second to hold himself together. It was obvious Ledger didn't take shit from Ry any longer.

Ry must have had some anger management classes because he let the statement stand. "From what I hear, you are too." His gaze swept down Kash's body, leaving no room to doubt the true reason he flagged Ledger down. Greed swam in his eyes.

Kash's mood swung wildly from enjoying watching Ledger make Ry squirm to ready to kill someone. "You have a schedule to keep." Kash kept the statement formal-sounding and directed solely at Ledger.

Relief touched his features at the out. He checked the time on his phone. "Damn. You're right." Ledger's gaze flickered toward Ry. "Sorry to keep things short, but I have to get moving."

Ry looked desperate to keep Ledger from getting away. "Okay. Yeah. We should catch up soon. It's been a long time."

Ledger nodded and gave an awkward wave as Kash steered him in the opposite direction. Kash didn't feel Ledger relax until they were out of Ry's sight.

"Thank you for that. I know you could've handled that a dozen other ways. But I've had all the drama I care to spare with Ry. Nowadays, I prefer not to see his face at all."

"It's all good. We're supposed to be having a fun day. Not a going to jail day."

Ledger's sexy chuckle washed away any bad juju left behind by Ry's presence.

"We should go get some real food to wash the taste of flavorless fried food from our mouths."

"Sounds good to me. Figure out where we're going before we reach the car, so I'll know which way to fight traffic."

Ledger huffed. "Already? Are we really going to toss the grenade back and forth on where to eat this soon in our relationship?"

"I don't even know what that means."

Ledger's gaze flashed with irritation. "Your giant, goofy smile says otherwise."

Kash paused, forcing the crowd to go around them like a boulder in the river. "I'm smiling because you make me deliriously happy."

Ledger looked as if he melted. "Same."

For a moment, they simply stared at each other. Kash cleared his throat. “What’s the name of that cafe with the frozen mugs?”

“Marge’s?”

Kash nodded and started guiding Ledger toward the SUV again. “That’s the place. Are they good?”

“Yeah. I just don’t come this way often.”

“Let’s go there.”

Ledger stepped closer. “Sounds great. Sorry I got irritated. I didn’t expect this day to take a terrible turn.”

“Don’t apologize. The last thing I wanted to do today was see Ry again.”

Ledger took his arm and squeezed. “I was talking about the cookie. Seeing Ry means less than nothing to me. I ended up with you. He ended up with no hair. Why should I be bitter?"

A loud laugh popped from Kash that made heads turn. He tried swallowing the sound. "Oh my god. I didn't even notice that. I was too busy trying to figure out what the hell was going on with his face."

Their laughter didn't stop until they were back inside the SUV. While they waited for the air to really get going in the California heat, they stared at each other. It felt like a thousand words were exchanged in the silence. Fate had really shown out when it put them together. Kash had never seen anything more beautiful.

They had a great day. When they got home, Ledger wasn't the least bit surprised when his phone rang. His only shock was that it was Valon and not Ry. He wasn't blind to how Ry had looked at him, and yuck.

Ledger damn near juggled his phone trying to answer as quickly as possible. It was rare as hell for Valon to call him first.

"Hello?"

"You'll never guess who called me?"

Ledger knew, but he loved the way Valon sounded, as if he had the hottest of teas to spill. “Who?”

“Ry. Actually, this is the second time in the last few weeks. I fully expected he wanted money. Nope. He’s obsessed with your being with Kash.”

Ledger didn’t know how to react.

Kash gave him a quick kiss and motioned toward the bedroom, silently mouthing, “I’m going to take a shower.”

Ledger nodded and then savored the show of Kash’s ass walking away from him. “Yeah. We ran into him today. He said he saw us a few weeks ago, but I can’t imagine where. I damn near get everything delivered these days, and I have my own gym. How have you been, by the way?”

"I'm the same as always. He said he was out jogging when he saw you two go into a storage unit."

Ledger nodded like Valon could see his head move. "Kash had his things in storage. I figured there was no reason for him to pay for a storage unit when he could just move his things here."

"Makes sense to me. What happened when you saw him today?"

Ledger moved to the couch and sat. "It was kind of weird, actually. He seemed off, twitchy and shit. Thankfully, Kash was quick on his toes to make an excuse to get me out of there. Ry kept looking at Kash and quickly looking away while acting all nervous and pretending he wasn't there."

"He's probably afraid Kash will tell you he had to start sleeping with a gun at our house because Ry wouldn't leave him alone at night."

Everything inside Ledger froze. He didn't know what to say. His brain completely locked up.

"Ah, damn. Let me call you back, Dad. It's always something around here."

Ledger spoke by rote. "Okay. I love you."

"You too."

Nothing but silence came through the line. Ledger still hadn't moved the phone from his ear. The doorbell rang. If he had been thinking clearly, he would have ignored it. Instead, his feet moved that way while his brain lagged like a computer with too many tabs open. He opened the door without checking the peephole. Ry stood on the other side. Something that had been brewing for more than a decade grew bigger by the second.

"Sorry to just drop by like this. I realized I don't have your number any longer, and I doubt Valon would give it to me." He looked right and left, admiring the house. "Damn. Valon really set you up here."

There was no way Ry didn't see the fury bleeding from every pore.

Ry shifted nervously. "Is it okay if I come in? There's something I'd like to talk to you about. Something long overdue."

"You're right. Some things are long overdue." Ledger's fist shot out, connecting solidly with Ry's eye. The second punch took him to his knees.

Ledger's chest heaved. He didn't feel better. He slammed the door and locked it. Ledger set the alarm because he wasn't completely out of his head. His knuckles bled from the force of the hit. Ledger didn't care. He headed straight for the bathroom inside the bedroom where Kash showered. Ledger jerked open the shower door. He hadn't calmed at all.

Kash's gaze shot toward the doorway. "Hey." His smile fell. "Holy shit, Ledge. What happened? You're bleeding."

Ledger stepped inside the shower fully dressed and backed Kash against the wall. "Don't you ever let anyone scare you the way you let Ry. You should've fucking told me the second he made you uncomfortable. I never would've let him stay in the same house as you."

"Whoa. Wait. Is this Ry's blood on your shirt? What the fuck happened in the last ten minutes?"

"Don't change the subject. Why didn't you tell me what Ry did?"

Guilt etched Kash's features. Thankfully, as always, Kash was honest. "Maybe you would've blamed me and not let me come back. Even if you didn't blame me, you definitely wouldn't have let me come back for my safety. Worse, maybe you would've thought I lied and want me out of your life. There's a lot I can handle, but never seeing you again, knowing you hate me, isn't one of those things. Now tell me why you're bleeding."

Ledger's hand shook as he touched Kash's cheek. His knuckles were split, and blood poured from the wounds. "I need you to trust me."

"I do." Kash looked hurt at even the insinuation.

Ledger dropped his forehead to Kash's chest and breathed in his existence. "Valon called and told me everything."

"Did you punch a hole in the wall, or teleport to Ry's?"

Ledger shuffled closer, still not giving a damn he was fully clothed. He couldn't lift his head. The weight of all the mistakes he had made weighed too heavily on him. "He's probably still on the front porch where I left him."

"Damn, baby." Kash's arms wrapped around Ledger and squeezed him. "He's not worth this."

That had Ledger's head shooting up. "No. But you are, and I never would've put you out for something he did. Maybe I stayed through a lot of shit, but it was never because I was desperate or weak. You're worth twenty of him."

Kash cupped Ledger's face between his hands. Like always, his piercing stare left Ledger feeling like they were alone in the world. "I love you."

Kash had said those words in anger and pleading but never so point-blank. His eyes said everything. He expected to hear them back. Kash needed to know how Ledger felt.

"I absolutely love you too." An embarrassed snort escaped Ledger. "You have no idea how badly I want to go back and finish the job. I'm so fucking in love with you. How dare he touch you?"

Kash captured his mouth in a scorching kiss, stopping the rage before it built again. He fought like hell to get Ledger out of his soaked clothes. While he had left his phone on the couch, his wallet hadn't dodged a shower. Ledger didn't give a shit about the ruined leather. He didn't care if every article of clothing was useless after tearing at them to make them go away. Everything inside him was a mess. Valon still didn't know about them, and Ledger was so in this relationship. He wanted a full life with Kash. Ledger couldn't lose this. He had never felt so close and strongly about anyone. Ledger wasn't scared about losing Kash. He already knew he wouldn't let that happen, and he had no idea what keeping this would do to the rest of his life. Ledger still wanted to go finish the job with Ry. Finding out Ry had tried to touch Kash in any way was a fire in his gut.

Ledger couldn't take it.

He dove his fingers into Kash's hair, forcing Kash to hold his stare. "You're mine. You've always been mine. Don't you ever let anyone make you feel any other way again."

Kash looked aroused as hell. Sexy as fuck. "Same. Anyone touches you and they're dead."

The moment their bare skin finally met, Ledger wanted to cry. This was his man. His other half. If they never left this shower, Ledger would live the happiest of lives.

They came together hard. Their tongues clashed and fought for dominance. Ledger's back hit the wall, and his feet left the floor. He had no clue what Kash found to use as lube, and they definitely didn't have a condom. There was no stopping this. They were too close to insanity.

When Kash shoved his way inside, Ledger gasped for air. Everything went still. Their gazes met. They didn't look away as Kash rolled his hips and took Ledger. Fuck, everything he did felt amazing. Kash knew how to play his body. As much as he wanted to savor the moment, his emotions were too high. He strained as much as he could, trying to take what he wanted. Kash lifted and lowered, fucking him hard. Kash sucked his neck and moaned. Ledger babbled with no clue what he said. He was pretty sure he begged for the dick.

Kash suddenly changed angles and hit the right spot. Cries reverberated from the walls as Ledger raced toward the edge.

"I fucking love you. I need to watch you come. Give it to me, sexy."

Ledger blew. He sucked air and gave no shits about how he looked. He was in the clouds. Kash moaned as he pumped inside Ledger. His thrusts slowed, and the air changed. Their mouths met again. Ledger's eyes burned at the power of the moment. They were forever, and it wouldn't be easy, but it would definitely be worth it.

Chapter Nine

No one could possibly know how much Kash hated leaving a sleeping Ledger behind. But Ajax had a job for Kash and Kash had to do what he had to do. This was life. Kash still worried Ledger would get sick of this at some point. He knew he was good. There was no danger on the horizon. Prince Noir had his back. He had complete faith in that, but what Ledger thought mattered. As those thoughts took hold, Kash pulled into the parking lot of the first grocery store he came to on his way home. His feet moved faster than necessary. Kash's heart raced. Panic pressed on his brain. Ledger couldn't give up on him. While Kash had lived his entire life having no one in his corner, Ledger had always been there until Kash had disappeared to save Ledger from him. Now Ledger was actually his, and he couldn't go back to an empty life. Kash just couldn't.

He headed straight for the flowers and grabbed the prettiest bouquet he saw. They didn't feel like enough. He eyed the balloons. None of them fit his purpose. His mind raced to think of what else he could do. He spotted a sign that marked the candy aisle. As he moved that way, he saw an end cap with sundae toppings. A smile stretched Kash's lips. Yeah. That was what he needed. He froze. Damn. He needed a cart or something. Kash backtracked and found a hand basket. He had to stack everything carefully inside, but he found every ingredient he could possibly need.

As he put the bags in the SUV, the hot fudge caught his attention. He froze. The past swept over him, unearthing a long-forgotten memory.

"I can't believe how much stuff you bought. Surely, this many toppings will make the ice cream inedible."

Ledger focused on Kash with a smile that made his breath catch. That had been happening all too often. Kash's chest hurt. He shouldn't beg the universe for the things that would never be, but here he was.

"You haven't had my famous sundae yet. I promise you'll love it."

Kash shrugged. "I've only had the hot fudge sundae at that carhop joint next to work. It probably won't take much to impress me." Plus, Kash always loved everything Ledger made for him.

Ledger stared at him in silence long enough he wished he hadn't admitted to that. Before Kash could ask him to forget he said anything, Ledger shook his head. "We definitely have to fix that. I promise it won't be inedible. The secret ingredient is love." He winked. It got harder for Kash to breathe.

"Yeah. I'd eat that."

They held each other's stare. Neither of them looked away, but they also didn't show an ounce of emotion.

The microwave dinged. "Shit. I forgot to stop this to check it every fifteen seconds." He grabbed a potholder and pulled the jar from the microwave. The glass container slipped from the slick glove and shattered on the floor, sending hot glass and lava-temperature fudge flying. Ledger jumped backward, narrowly escaping the splatter.

Kash flew into action. He threw his arm out in front of Ledger, physically pushing Ledger away from the mess. "I've got this. Don't move. I don't want you to cut your feet." Once he was certain Ledger wouldn't move, Kash rushed to put on his shoes. After stomping into his work boots, he grabbed the broom. Kash immediately set to work, making sure not a single sliver of glass stayed behind. He glanced up and found Ledger watching him with an expression Kash didn't understand.

With his elbows braced on the countertop, Ledger rolled a glass container between his hands. When Kash caught him staring, Ledger held up the jar. "It's a good thing I bought two." They burst into laughter. Kash had no idea why, but—as always with Ledger—he was having a great time. He never wanted the night to end.

Kash still felt the same way every day with Ledger. He couldn't let that end.

Ledger stood inside the refrigerator door and zoned out. He wanted something, but he didn't know what. There was a craving he couldn't place. Kash was gone, and Ledger felt aimless. Maybe if he ate something sweet, he would be satisfied. Something just felt off.

The back door opened, and Kash came through the door. He toed off his shoes. Ledger eyed the gorgeous bouquet of various flowers and bags of groceries hooked on his arm. Kash kept his gaze locked on his feet.

“On the way home, I realized I really need to get another car. If anything happens while I’m out, you won’t have anything but my old car. I can’t have that.”

He looked up.

Ledger watched his every move.

Kash smiled. “Hey, baby. I got you flowers.”

A smile exploded across Ledger’s face. “I was hoping those were for me.”

Kash looked confused. “Who else would they be for?”

A chuckle rumbled from Ledger. “You really need to learn when I’m joking.”

Kash’s expression cleared. “Oh, sorry.”

Ledger furrowed his brow. "Is everything okay?"

Kash closed the distance between them and stole a kiss. "Come see what else I got."

Ledger didn't press. Kash had always fought against dark thoughts. Ledger pushing wouldn't help anything. Kash needed happiness to dissipate the ugliness.

"What did you get? I was just searching for something."

Kash set everything on the island.

Ledger joined him and smelled the flowers. He spun the vase, looking at the bouquet from every direction. "These are beautiful. Thank you." His gaze caught on the items Kash pulled from the bag.

"Oh, my god. It's like you read my mind. I haven't eaten a sundae in years." The dessert reminded him too much of Kash. Now he couldn't wait to dive in.

Kash pulled two jars of hot fudge from the bag.

Ledger burst into laughter.

Kash flashed him a smile. "Just in case."

Ledger shook his head. "I'll never live down that destruction."

In a move Ledger didn't see coming, Kash suddenly plucked Ledger from his feet and set him on the counter next to his haul. He pulled Ledger to the edge and stood between Ledger's knees. His gaze never moved from holding Ledger's stare. "I can't eat ice cream anymore without remembering how badly I wanted to eat that sundae off your sexy body."

Ledger licked his lips nervously. Sometimes, Kash was more intense than usual. Ledger couldn't stop himself from embracing the fact he had wanted the same thing. "Do it."

A heartbeat passed. Kash snatched the bags and Ledger. Ledger wrapped his legs around Kash and hung on for the ride. When Kash lowered him onto the bed, Ledger scrambled out of his clothes while Kash stripped. Once they were nude, they dove into the bags.

Ledger found the whipped cream first. "Hell yeah." He squirted Kash's cock as fast as possible so he could get the drop on Kash. Ledger had Kash's dick in his mouth before Kash could react.

"Fuck." Kash grabbed his hair. For a second, Ledger thought Kash might pull away. Instead, his grip tightened. "Damn. I can't let it go down like this." He gently pushed Ledger away. "We're in this together."

Ledger watched Kash twist the lid off a caramel jar. He didn't hesitate to slide back and make room for Kash to sit on his face. "Yes. I want it."

Kash passed Ledger the whipped cream he abandoned. Once Ledger was settled, Kash straddled him where Ledger could do whatever he wanted. Kash poured caramel over Ledger's hard cock, making him squirm. "Delicious."

The sexy way that word left Kash's lips had him poised on the edge of a knife. He always felt like Kash would make him come in two seconds. Ledger wasn't going down alone.

Kash sucked Ledger's dick, like he wanted every drop of that caramel. Ledger didn't need more whipped cream. He had Kash down his throat.

Kash moaned around Ledger's cock. Ledger lifted his hips, chasing the sound. Kash whimpered, and suddenly, Ledger had all the patience in the world. Before the end of the night, they would have to throw these bed coverings away, and Ledger would taste every item in those bags on Kash's body. This was his version of heaven. He could spend eternity right here.

Chapter Ten

KASH: *I HAD TO run out. If you wake up before I get home, text me if you want me to pick up anything while I'm out.*

Kash: *Never mind. I'm bringing home breakfast. Do not move from that bed. I'm feeding you.*

Ledger: *I'm finished recording. You can stop hiding in the bedroom.*

Kash: *It's not hiding if I'm working on a new comic strip. I get engrossed and forget time exists.*

Ledger: *I'll come to you then.*

Kash: *I made you a cozy spot right next to me.*

Ledger: *Why do I get the feeling you won't get any more drawings done?*

Kash: *We'll see.*

Kash: *I'm always throwing every soap and bead into this washer. Help!*

Ledger: *I'm on my way. This isn't a trap, is it? We'll actually be doing laundry, right?*

Kash: **evil smile* Come find out, my pretty.*

Ledger*: I love you.*

Kash*: I love you too. You know I'm right beside you on the couch, right?*

Ledger: *And?*

Kash: *You're right.*

From his spot on a lounge by the pool, Kash watched Ledger man the grill. His white hair captured the sun. A sheen of sweat coated his cut body. Fuck. He was beautiful. Ledger glanced his way and winked. Kash melted inside. He felt like a kid with a crush all over again. It never got old, looking at Ledger with stars in his eyes.

Ledger motioned his way with the spatula. "You look overheated. It'll be a couple of minutes longer on these burgers. Jump in the pool and cool off."

Oh, he was overheated all right. Kash stood. "Sounds like a solid plan, since watching you has me hot as hell."

The way Ledger smiled was everything. "Damn. Of all the times to forget to wear my *Kiss the Cook* apron."

Kash changed directions and overcame Ledger. Ledger laughed until Kash's mouth covered his, cutting off the sound. Their kiss turned scorching before Kash could reel it in.

Ledger jumped back. "Goddamn it!"

Kash immediately went on alert as Ledger eyed his arm. "What happened?" An ugly red mark appeared on Ledger's arm. "Holy shit. Are you okay? What can I do?"

Ledger looked a little embarrassed. "I bumped it on the grill. It's okay. I'm good."

Kash was on the verge of hyperventilating. He couldn't bear to see Ledger hurt. "Fuck that. Tell me what to do. Let me get your first-aid kit. Just tell me where it is? I've never noticed one. Shit. Why don't you have a first-aid kit?"

Ledger cupped Kash's face, forcing Kash to hold his gaze, as if centering him. "I'm fine. It's not that bad. If you need to do something just to ease your mind, *our* first-aid kit is in the cabinet next to the refrigerator."

Nothing could have calmed him quicker than Ledger calling something theirs.

Once he took one calming breath, the rest came smoother. It hit him. Kash never panicked. Not about anything. He had lived through a lot of traumatic events and simply carried on. But this was Ledger, and Kash couldn't take it.

Kash blew out a slow breath. "Sorry. I don't know what happened there. I'll get the first-aid kit." He tried to turn away.

Ledger stopped him from leaving. "Do you mind taking these burgers off the grill instead? The heat hitting this burn is worse than anything."

Kash immediately jumped in to do whatever Ledger needed.

Ledger pressed his lips against the spot between Kash's shoulder blades as he passed. "You're the sexiest man I've ever set eyes on, and still you managed to somehow look even hotter by worrying about me. I haven't gotten much of that in my life."

Kash's heart melted and hardened at the same time. He couldn't explain that one. All he knew was he loved knowing he brought something to the table no one else had, but Ledger deserved so much better than he had gotten.

"I'm sure it's not easy being the one who worries and takes care of everyone else. If no one else has realized how blessed they are to have you, just know I see it." Kash had kept his gaze on taking care of the grill and burgers before turning Ledger's way. He had worried he might show how angry he was about Ry all over again. Now he needed Ledger to see the truth in Kash's eyes while Kash continued. "You're amazing, and I don't deserve to have you in my life. That doesn't mean I'll set you free. I'm too selfish for that, but I know I'm damn lucky to be here. Even if I fail at everything else in life, you'll know I have your back every day." Sometimes even Kash didn't know where he was going with his ramblings. He didn't know how to vocalize the way Ledger's existence in his life had always been priceless to him.

Ledger kissed the corner of Kash's mouth. His lips lingered.

Kash closed his eyes and savored the experience, stashing it away to be one of his favorite moments. There was more to them than sexual attraction. Even though Kash had known that, he felt it in that moment in a way he hadn't before. Ledger's kiss showed his heart. He truly intended for this to be a real relationship. No going back. Ledger's sweet kiss felt like forever. Kash fought the urge to cry. One thing he had always known was Ledger could crush him like nothing had ever done before. Even before Kash had caught himself thinking about Ledger's mouth in a way he shouldn't, Ledger had been a steady presence that Kash had needed with a desperation he couldn't put into words. He knew what he had to lose, and he couldn't do it.

Ledger took a step back, but the spell he cast lingered. "Put those on the table. I'll run in and swipe some burn cream on this arm. Then I'll bring out the rest of the food."

"I can help." He wanted to stay glued to Ledger's side. He felt oddly vulnerable now. But the love in Ledger's eyes was real. It was his.

Ledger chuckled. "Go sit down."

Kash watched Ledger head inside the house with hope filling him to the brim. He genuinely had a real home now. A place for him in the world existed, and it was right here. Kash terrified himself, knowing how far he would go to keep this. He would burn the world.

At the kitchen counter, cold water poured onto his burn. It didn't hurt that bad. Ledger just got lost in his head while staring out the window above the sink. He wasn't torn. Ledger didn't have a tough decision ahead of him. This was his life. *His*. He wanted to cry with relief at the revelation. The way Kash had reacted to seeing him hurt was a stone crushing his chest. Love pressed so hard on him that he couldn't breathe.

He caught sight of Kash inside the screen in eating area by the pool. Kash kept moving the plate of hamburgers from one spot to the next. A lump formed in his throat. Goddamn. Four months of being the one cared for, saving him from having to be the one who always managed everything, sigh. He couldn't even describe how much lighter he felt. In fact, Ledger might have turned into a bit of a princess. That was how accustomed he had become to being pampered by Kash. It was too adorable watching Kash try to decide where Ledger would sit, so he would have the best angle to reach the burgers. There were only two of them. They could both reach them fine. Damn. He was so fucking in love. Ledger wanted to ask what he had done to deserve this miracle. Unfortunately, Ledger knew he didn't deserve this. He could never tell his story about falling for Kash without looking terrible. Some things in life didn't give a damn about anyone's feelings. Love was one of those things. It was all the same, whether it was falling in love or losing it; no one had any real control. Some stories weren't beautiful or tragic. They just were what they were. Kash and he felt inevitable.

Ledger turned off the water and found the first-aid kit. Suddenly, he couldn't get back outside to be with Kash fast enough. He needed to make up for those five years they missed, even though things wouldn't be what they were right now if he had turned his life upside down earlier.

He ran around grabbing everything they needed for their burgers. Ledger had several bottles tucked under his arm, along with buns and chips. Plus, the plates of toppings in his hand. He waddled outside, trying not to drop anything.

At the first sight of him, Kash laughed. He jumped in to help Ledger carry everything to the table. "I offered to help." Humor laced the reminder. Kash rescued what he could, freeing Ledger.

Ledger couldn't stop smiling. He felt a little ridiculous about his desperate race to get back to Kash. He was so sexy, though. Wearing nothing but his swimming trunks, Kash's every tattoo was on display. The way they moved with his muscles made Ledger weak. As they stood side by side, setting everything on the table, Ledger couldn't take it anymore. "You're really fucking gorgeous. You know that, right?"

"It doesn't matter if I know it." He glanced over and met Ledger's stare. "All that matters is if you think so. I'll get older and change too."

"You'll always be beautiful to me."

Kash quickly kissed his nose. "Same. I love you."

That never got old. "I love you too."

"*Fuck*, it's hot out here." Valon came tumbling out the back door. Sunglasses on and dressed all in black like it wasn't August. "I hope you made enough for..." He glanced behind him. "Well, hell. Where did my guard go?" Valon shrugged. "Guess it's just me."

Ledger went on full alert. He couldn't believe how close they had come to getting caught. Not that he didn't want Valon to know. He just hadn't found the right words yet, and he sure as hell didn't want Valon to find out on his own.

Ledger's smile was real, though. It was rare for Valon to pop in like this. "There's always enough for you." Especially since Ledger had made enough to have leftovers. He always did, just in case. Hope sprang eternal.

“Nice.” Valon chose a chair and sat. He took the one next to Kash and grabbed a paper plate.

Ledger felt the way Kash avoided looking too closely at either of them. Awkwardness settled in. Ledger did his best to keep the tension out of the air. “I’m glad to see you.”

Valon doctored his burger like he didn’t think Ledger meant him.

This time, Kash and he exchanged glances.

Kash jumped in. “I would’ve thought you’d be halfway across the country right now.”

With the way his chin shot up and his head turned Kash’s way, Valon seemed surprised anyone spoke to him. “I don’t actually know what day it is. But I'm pretty sure this is one of the weeks I have off."

"That's awesome. I love seeing you." Ledger sat across from the pair, smiling too brightly, and desperately trying to break the tension coiling inside him. "Eat as much as you'd like."

Valon lifted one shoulder in a half shrug. "I'm really not all that hungry. You know I can't resist your cooking, though." He took a bite of his burger. It looked as if he stared into space. Unfortunately, Ledger couldn't get a good read on Valon with the dark sunglasses in place. They ate in uncomfortable silence. Kash was always the one who made everyone laugh at the dinner table. Now he kept his gaze locked on his plate. Ledger couldn't stop glancing between the two. Either Kash didn't look his way because he didn't want to give them away, or Ledger hurt him with his silence.

Ledger rubbed his chest. He knew whichever way he went right now, he would hurt someone. If he didn't speak up right now, it would be worse later. Either Valon would think he lied and kept secrets or Kash would get fed up and leave.

He took a deep breath. "There's something I need to—"

Kash's chin shot up.

Valon's cellphone rang, cutting off Ledger. Valon moved his sunglasses to the top of his head. His eyes were blood red and red-rimmed. They had black blotches underneath them. "There's the party police known as my bodyguard." He answered, "Hello?" The shout coming through the phone had Valon jerking the phone away from his ear for a second. “Dang, dude. Take it down a notch. You know I’m an adult, right? Plus, you work for me, not the other way around.” Valon pushed away from the table and walked away before the true yelling match began.

Kash and Ledger held each other’s stare. A silent message passed between them, and their feet brushed beneath the table as if reassuring each other. Today wasn’t the day. Valon already had enough going on. They might not know what it was, but they couldn’t add to it.

Chapter Eleven

Shadows of leaves danced between the strips of light on the ceiling from the window blinds. Kash had no idea what time it was, but he knew he had slept much later than usual. His muscles ached from the massive workout Ledger had put him through the entire night. Between being in the sun all day yesterday and the way he had serviced Ledger last night, he had fallen asleep in total exhaustion. Kash stretched. He knew Ledger wasn't there without looking. There was an emptiness to the room only Ledger's presence could fill.

Kash rolled out of the bed and padded to the bathroom. He rushed through the usual morning pee and teeth brushing. Kash found a discarded pair of pajama pants and went in search of Ledger. A bright smile lit his face when he saw Ledger sitting at the kitchen island with his entire recording setup. For whatever reason, Ledger always slipped away to do these videos, like it embarrassed him to have an audience. He looked sexy in nothing but shorts and an apron. Ledger spoke softly and held up various vegetables and kitchen utensils. Kash couldn't take it. He sneaked across the room and then pounced. Kash snagged Ledger's jaw and tilted his head back, cutting off his words with a scorching kiss.

He pulled away and brushed noses with Ledger. “There’s the love of my life.”

Ledger blinked, looking stunned. “I love you too. Um, I’m on live.”

It took a second for the words to penetrate before the horror set in. “Fuck.” His shock wouldn’t abate. No way would he have done that on purpose. “I’m sorry.” The apology came from his soul. He didn’t know if this would go straight to Valon. Most likely. Kash would never have chosen for Valon to find out this way. He quickly backed out of camera view.

Still wearing his open shock, Ledger’s gaze slid back to the phone clipped to a ring light. He cleared his throat. “Sorry about that. That's about all for my lesson today. Thank you all for hanging out with me. Until next time." Ledger killed the feed and stared into space.

"Holy shit, Ledge. I never would've done that had I known. Will this get straight back to Valon? What can I do? How can I fix this?"

Ledger cleared his throat. While still visibly reeling, Ledger focused on him. "It's fine. I'll call Valon. It's time we talked anyway. I don't want him to think I'm hiding things from him. For real, I don't know what to say, though. I don't know how he'll react."

Kash was furious with himself. He felt like he had betrayed Ledger, taking away Ledger's right to handle things his way. Kash swiped his hand over his eyes and paced away. “Fuck! I’m so... ugh. You deserved better from me.”

Ledger stood and wrapped his arms around Kash, stopping his crash out. “Today is no better or worse to do this. He’s always needed to be told.”

Ledger didn’t understand. Kash knew this was the end of them. He knew as soon as Valon snapped, Ledger would walk away from them.

The pain was nearly his undoing. He held Ledger’s stare. Kash knew Ledger had to see his heart breaking. “I’m not ready. When I woke up, all I could think about was finding you so I could touch you again. There’s no way I could’ve known it would be my last time. I’m not ready,” he repeated. That was one point he couldn’t drive home hard enough. He didn't know how to lose Ledger, but he would.

Ledger's expression and voice became comforting. "Stop. Valon is a grown man with his own life. I'm allowed to have one of those too, and you're it. You're the life I want. When I say I love you, I mean it. I can't let you go. We just—" Ledger's phone rang, cutting him off. He glanced toward the device, looking resigned.

Kash took a step back. "Not answering will only make it worse."

With a nod, Ledger headed for the phone. He stared at the face as he removed it from the ring light. "I don't recognize the number, but he might be calling from anywhere." Ledger didn't hesitate. He looked determined. Thankfully, he answered on speaker so Kash wasn't left out.

"Hello?"

"You slimy son of a bitch. How could you do this to our son?"

Ledger pinched the spot between his eyes. "So much for you not knowing my number."

"Really? That's what you have to say right now."

This entire conversation was rich as hell, considering Ry had already gotten his ass handed to him over trying to fuck Kash. Now he had the nerve to lecture Ledger.

"Does Valon even know? Don't answer that. I know he doesn't. Don't worry. I'll fix that." The phone call disconnected before either of them could speak.

Ledger tossed him a defeated look.

Kash didn't know what to do, but he knew Ledger couldn't let Ry get to Valon first. "Call him. Don't let Ry make things seem worse than they are—like you're a liar or something. He could spin shit any way he wants. Get to Valon first."

Ringing came through the speaker before the words finished falling from Kash's lips, proving they were on the same page. Ledger was already calling Valon. It rang several times before going to voicemail. "Yo. You know what to do?"

Ledger didn't hesitate. "I don't know if any rumors have reached you yet, but please call me. Ry has already called here, making threats. Please don't let him twist things. Call me." He hit end and covered his face with both hands.

Kash stood by feeling helpless.

Ledger dropped his hands and looked up, blinking at the ceiling like trying to get himself under control.

Kash couldn't take it. "Tell me what to do. I'll do anything."

When Ledger looked his way, he looked defeated. "There's nothing to do. All we can do is wait." Ledger's gaze moved to the phone. He bit the side of thumbnail.

In this, Kash had no patience. He couldn't sit back and wait to see if they were over. Ledger said that wouldn't happen, but there was one thing Ledger hadn't considered. Kash wouldn't let Ledger choose him. He loved Ledger too much to be the reason Valon walked away. Kash already knew Valon had no problem turning his back on anyone at any time. Maybe he still answered when Ry called sometimes, but Kash didn't doubt that man hadn't seen Valon since the day he left. He had easily walked away from years with Kash when Kash had always had his back. As much as Kash couldn't picture Valon never speaking to Ledger again, it might happen.

Kash moved to hold Ledger. He kissed Ledger's forehead. "Go take a shower, baby. I'll stand guard over your phone and rush it to the bathroom if Valon calls. Sitting here making yourself sick won't help anything."

Ledger nodded. "Okay. I guess I can't choose to never shower again, waiting for a call that might not come."

Kash kissed him again and nudged him toward their bedroom.

Ledger headed down the hall. It looked as if every one of his muscles were tensed.

Kash counted to twenty after Ledger went into the bedroom to grab Ledger's phone. Thankfully, this wasn't the first time he had unlocked the device, except on those times Ledger had been there. Kash didn't feel guilty. This was an emergency. He quickly found Valon's location. He zoomed in to see the exact street Valon was on in Los Angeles. As soon as he had it, Ledger flew into high gear. He threw some clothes on, sneaked Ledger's phone into the bathroom so he wouldn't miss any calls and made some calls of his own. He phoned in every favor he could. Kash had the resources to find an exact address at the drop of a hat. To his absolute relief, a part-time guard showed up right on time to give Kash the day off.

Kash nodded at the guy. "Ledger is in the shower. When he comes out, tell him I had to run out for something, but I'll be back later."

The dark-haired guy—whose name Kash couldn't even remember due to all the stress—nodded along. "No problem. Have a good day. I've got things under control."

Kash knew he did. He would never leave Ledger with someone who couldn't handle the job. In record time, Kash was behind the wheel of Ledger's SUV. It took a little under three hours to drive from Santa Maria to L.A., and that was if traffic was light. He needed to break every speed limit. There was business to settle.

As Ledger stepped out of the shower, the first thing he saw was his phone. That was odd. He checked the device. No missed calls or texts had come through while he showered. Ledger dried off, overthinking everything except for why Kash had brought him the phone. Kash probably had to use the restroom or something. No big deal.

Several times as he dressed, he paused and stared at nothing, making the chore take twice as long. As much as he searched his heart, Ledger couldn't find an excuse for himself. All he could think about was who Valon was now and compare it to the issue. He had no idea how Valon would react.

If Ledger was an absolute piece of shit and let anything happen with Kash back when they got nothing but silence from Valon, things would be different. Valon would and should have cut Ledger out of his life so fast, his head would still be spinning. Now, it felt like everyone involved were different people. No matter what, Ledger would never have chosen for Valon to find out this way. He couldn't apologize enough for that.

While fidgeting with his phone, Ledger made his way to the kitchen. He would make some tea and calmly find something to do to busy his mind. Ledger had just taken a shower, but maybe he should work out to break the stress.

As he stepped into the kitchen, Ledger found Marc sitting at the island and playing on his phone. The sight confused him for a second before he remembered today was officially one of Kash's days off. He really needed to let Steel know he only needed occasional security when Kash had something else to do. That was another mark against him. Valon had been paying for his ex to sleep with Ledger. Actually, he paid Steel, and Steel paid Kash. Technicalities didn't mean shit under the circumstances.

"Hey. I forgot you worked today. Have you seen Kash?"

Marc set his phone aside and focused on Ledger. He had Hawaiian blue eyes that were arresting. They kept people holding eye contact simply because they couldn't look away. "Hey. Kash went out. He said to tell you he needed to grab something, and he'll be back later."

Ledger tried not to show any of the feelings he couldn't control. Since he hadn't wanted Kash to see how upset he really was, so he wouldn't continue thinking they were over, his feelings couldn't be hurt from being left without Kash's support.

Instead, he shoved his phone in his back pocket and moved to the sink. He filled the kettle. "Would you like some tea?"

Marc chuckled. "It depends. Iced tea, yes. Hot tea, no. I know that's weird, but there's a difference, and it's vast."

The humor in Marc's voice made Ledger smile despite the war raging inside him. He spoke while he worked. "It's not weird. There is a difference. My son is the same way. I'll take tea however, but I got into the habit of only making iced tea, since I knew he'd be the one who drank the whole damn pitcher before anyone else got any."

Marc chuckled. "I've guarded a lot of powerful people but never anyone as famous as your son. What's it like knowing you raised a rock star?"

Ledger glanced up, smiling. "I'm extremely proud of him. It warms my entire soul to see him on stage with a full arena of people singing along with him. I can't even imagine how he feels standing up there. All the years of musical training, just him and me traveling to various competitions. Fame didn't land on him. He earned it. But yeah, I watch him and think, 'I made that.' It leaves me in awe, really." Ledger's throat swelled. He stared at nothing. "I suppose Kash and I trained him to leave us."

"Kash?"

Ledger shook his head slightly, shaking off the horrible memory of Valon stepping into fame and out of their lives. "Yeah." He tried not to get lost in his thoughts again. He cleared his throat. "Yeah. We've known Kash for years. Valon worked hard as hell to get where he is, but Kash and I pushed and shoved until he made it. There were a lot of times he wanted to give up, especially since singing and dancing around in front of a crowd went totally against his personality. He was sweet and extremely shy. Kash refused to let him cave because of that." A smile popped to his lips and fell again. He absentmindedly got the kettle going while his mind put together a few pieces. Kash had never let Valon shirk any type of duty. He hadn't let Valon leave Ledger behind back then when the fame first took hold. Kash wouldn't let Valon do it now either.

"Excuse me." Ledger walked away, pulling his cellphone from his back pocket as he went. He pulled up Kash's name before shutting himself in the bedroom. Ledger hit the call icon the moment he was alone. He paced as his call went unanswered. Voicemail answered, and

Ledger wanted to puke. The only reason Kash wouldn't answer was if he didn't want to lie to Ledger about where he was. Ledger ended the call and switched to checking the location of his SUV in comparison to Valon's phone. Valon was home in L.A., and Ledger's SUV was directly on the path to him. Ledger had thought there was no way this situation could get worse. He had been wrong.

Chapter Twelve

WIND CAUSED RIPPLES TO form on the water. Valon watched the clear surface dance. They hadn't owned a pool growing up. He had always wanted one, but Ry had always refused. Now Valon owned several located on various properties. He could build one right next to the one in front of him, if he liked. There was nothing stopping him. Honestly, that was one of his biggest flaws. Valon could do whatever and whomever he wanted. Until he couldn't. There were definitely a few exceptions to what he could buy. Topping that list, happiness, which was bullshit, by the way. People always said that, and it sounded like a load of crap. It was, just not in the way he always suspected.

Valon's family hadn't been poor growing up. He had been given access to a lot of advantages other kids didn't have. Yet his dads hadn't turned their noses up at the less fortunate. Well, his dad hadn't. He didn't know about Ry. They hadn't spent much time together over the years. Ry had been the absent parent, always working. Valon snorted. Yeah, working his way through every gym hottie he saw. To this day, Valon believed that was the biggest reason Ry had wanted to open his own gym. It was a hunting ground. So, really. Valon had only one parent. He had to think about anything at all other than what he couldn't have. Some days were harder than others. The shittiest part was no one could ever know it, because he was a goddamn star. How dare he experience anything other than absolute happiness? This career had taken him to some real heights, but the lows felt deeper than ever.

His phone rang incessantly, driving him insane. He checked the face. It was Ry again. Valon snapped and answered out of pure spite. "Stop fucking calling me, Ry. You're no longer my dad. You're not part of my life any longer. In fact, you're no fucking body to me but the loser who never deserved the family you had. I don't want you. Dad doesn't want you. For fuck's sake, catch a clue and go away." He disconnected the call before Ry said a word. If he called again, Valon might toss his phone in the pool. He might anyhow. Valon was so fucking sick of everything. He had tried blocking Ry a million times, but he always found a way to get to Valon. All he wanted was money. He didn't give a fuck about Valon. Never had.

"This place suits you. An awesome house for a badass superstar."

Valon looked over as Kash's voice cut through his thoughts. Sure enough. There Kash was, looking exactly how Valon had imagined he would look someday. Big and tattooed, with a smile that screamed he would do all the bad things.

"I'd ask how you got past security, but you probably know at least one of them."

Kash didn't look the least bit repentant when he sat sideways on the lounge next to Valon, facing him with his elbows braced on his knees. "You're ignoring calls and texts again."

Thank fuck he wore sunglasses. There was no stopping his eye roll. Some things about Kash never changed. He had acted more like Valon's father than anything else he had ever been to Valon.

"God forbid I take a single fucking second for myself to just think. Jesus Christ. This world is exhausting."

Kash openly studied him. "You sound almost as bitter as I am."

"Nope. I'm a rock star, remember? What could I possibly be bitter about?"

"Oh, I don't know. Maybe the fact that I'm dating your dad."

Valon made a dismissive gesture. "Oh, that. Who do you think put you two together?"

Kash scratched his chin. If Valon didn't know him so well, he would say Kash was unbothered. That chin scratch was a tell, though. He was nervous.

Valon sighed. Maybe this was exactly the distraction needed. "Look, you've always been better matched with Dad than me. I can fully admit that I'm a spoiled taker who—though I didn't realize it at the time—used you for the way you praised me. That's a bad description, but it doesn't matter anymore." Valon swiped his hand through the air, trying to wipe away the words. "I left you two alone for three whole months, for God's sake, and still you chased after me, hoping we weren't over. I realized then that neither of you were the type to hurt me by getting together, so I shrugged everything off and stayed my course. But then, Dad never dated and looked like a kicked puppy every time I saw him because I'm really all he has. I love him. He's my dad. I'd never hurt him if I could help it, but I have a super busy career now. I'm grown. My life can't revolve around him, and his life shouldn't revolve around me. It's his time to be free. So I called Steel and asked him to do whatever it took to get you to take on the job of guarding Dad. Granted, I told him it was because Dad wouldn't likely accept the protection he needed under any other circumstance, and Steel said he couldn't make any promises. But here you are and damn, dude. Who do you think turned off the alarm and worried you into sleeping in Dad's bed that first night? No one knows you two better than I do. I knew there was no way you two could resist each other a second time around."

Kash didn't look relieved. In fact, Valon wondered if Kash counted inside his head to gather every ounce of patience he possessed. "So you knew what you were doing back then. You hadn't just gotten carried away and overwhelmed and forgotten to keep in touch."

They weren't questions, so Valon didn't answer.

Kash pinched the spot between his eyes before he spoke again. When he focused on Valon again, his eyes were cold. "Here's the thing. You never deserved me."

Valon nodded. "Fair. You were owed that one."

Kash didn't stop. "Ledger deserves better than you."

"Ouch." Seriously, Kash might have earned a free shot at him, but his dad had been given the world from Valon. "I think you're forgetting how much I've given him over the years. He never has to want for a single thing."

"Oh, I know," Kash said, sounding beyond sarcastic. "You've given him all the space and anxiety. He's watched you turn into a stranger. On top of that, you forget he exists half the damn time." Kash paused, took a deep breath, and visibly reeled his temper in. Unfortunately, his next words hit so hard, he couldn't breathe. "Silence is its own type of violence, Valon. It's cruel and childish. It drives me fucking crazy the way you use it to punish everyone in your path. I know my ending up with your dad probably makes me look like a total piece of shit, but fuck, Valon. Back then, I loved you. Still do. Just in a different way and the way you just—" Kash snapped his teeth together and ran a hand through his hair as if thinking about pulling it out.

Valon wasn't dumb. He saw Kash's speech was really about Kash's feelings and not his dad's. Sometimes, it was just easier to pretend nothing hurt. Kash's entire life had tried to break him. He couldn't show weakness. It was too ingrained in him to carry the weight of everything.

"Do you think it was easy for me to watch you fall in love with my dad?"

Kash winced before guilt etched his features.

Valon didn't stop. "I mean, I get it. Your life was heavy and unstable. No one sat and listened to what you were dealing with. I don't know why I was like that. You have no idea how many times I've wondered why I never asked questions. Why didn't I know you as well as you knew me? How did I not even know what your dreams were? But I was young. Most everyone is a little selfish when they're young, except for you, of course, obviously."

"You're still young."

"So are you."

Kash snorted at his rebuttal.

“Yeah,” Valon said with all the sarcasm he could muster. “Now you know how you sounded. However, my point is, I had to sit with the knowledge that I had been such a bad person I drove my dad and boyfriend into each other’s arms. But you’re better with him, and he’s better with you, and I really don’t matter at all. But don’t you dare think I wasn’t hurt because I was, and yeah. I still fucking love you too, but in a different way. You were my best friend. My only friend, and now I don’t have any goddamn body.” By the time he was finished, Valon was yelling. Life was fucking killing him, and no one noticed. He couldn’t deal with this bullshit too.

“You have your dad, and you have me.” Kash sounded so fucking honest and caring that his tone had Valon fighting tears.

"Get changed and pack a bag. You're coming home for a few days. I know your schedule is a nightmare, but I can afford to fly you out with security to wherever you're going next. But right now, you need to be with us."

Fucking sunglasses. They weren't doing their job now. He felt the tears roll down his cheeks. Valon sniffed. "Am I paying you that good?"

A smile exploded across Kash's face. "You're not paying me at all. I called Steel and had myself dropped from the payroll and the entire contract moved to auto-pay from my account. I'm taking care of Ledger's protection."

Valon stood and gathered his towel. "Damn, Kash. Seriously, how are you affording all this?"

"I'm an enforcer for a drug lord."

A loud laugh burst from Valon. Kash was one of the funniest and greatest people he had ever known. He really missed having Kash's friendship, especially since he needed it now more than ever.

If there wasn't a hole in the floor yet, there would be in about two more turns of pacing. He had checked Kash's location a million times, so he knew Kash was almost home. Valon's location had stopped showing almost four hours earlier. Either Valon broke the last connection he had by stopping his sharing on the family app or he had turned off his phone. Either way, there was no way that was a good sign. Kash should have let Ledger handle this. Valon was his son. He needed to be the one trying to save them.

By the time Kash came through the door, Ledger was ready to fight him. He opened his mouth to blast Kash. Ledger gave no shits Marc was there. But then Valon dragged a suitcase through the door right behind Kash and Ledger's brain froze.

"You're here."

Valon looked up from the chore of getting his suitcase's wheels unstuck from the small lip right inside the doorway. "Hey. Yeah. I've come to visit for a little while, if that's okay?" His expression turned unsure, as if he should have called before he came. "I have someone coming with my car tomorrow, so you don't have to taxi me around or anything like that."

Ledger crossed the room and hugged Valon. He couldn't believe how much Valon honestly believed he was a burden to Ledger. The truth dripped from every sad note. "You never have to ask permission. As long as I live, any place I live is your home too. I'm your dad."

To his surprise, Valon hugged him back as if he needed Ledger's love. "Thanks."

Ledger fought a wave of unexpected tears. He couldn't let them fall. "You never have to thank me either."

“Sure I do. I was raised to say please and thank you.”

With a chuckle, Ledger helped Valon get his suitcase inside. He chanced a glance Kash’s way. Kash was busy talking to Marc about them getting together tomorrow about some job opportunity. Meanwhile, Ledger desperately wanted to know how Kash had done this. Then again, maybe Valon still didn’t know about them. There was a slim possibility Valon hadn’t heard, especially if Valon ignored Ry’s calls the same way he did Ledger’s.

“Let me just stick this thing in my room, and I’ll be back.”

There was a room he considered his. Ledger’s heart melted. He nodded and watched Valon head down the hall. The moment he was out of view and earshot, Ledger looked Kash's way and stage whispered, "How did you do this?"

Kash winked. "I told him to grab his shit and get in the car."

Ledger shook his head.

Valon reappeared before Ledger could get any more information. "What's for dinner? I feel like I haven't eaten in ages."

Ledger headed straight for the fridge. "Well, let's figure it out."

As they hovered together inside the open refrigerator, Valon slipped beneath his arm and held his waist the way he used to do when he was little. Ledger's eyes stung. It was as if a switch flipped inside him. Their biggest problem wasn't Valon's behavior as much as it was Ledger's inability to let go. There hadn't been a smooth transition from child to adult. It felt like Valon had been ripped from him in one fast move.

Ledger pressed his lips to Valon's temple. "Have I told you lately how proud I am that you're my son?"

"I'm sure you have, but I always love hearing it."

Ledger chuckled. "Tell me what you want to eat, and I'll make it happen."

Valon looked like the kid he remembered when he smiled. "Oooh. Do you know that spicy hamburger soup thing you used to make?"

"Yep."

"Let's do that."

Ledger backed away. "I'm on it. Likely, I'll have to get a rush grocery delivery, but it still won't take long." As he pulled his phone from his back pocket to do exactly what he claimed, a text appeared.

Kash: *He knows everything and is completely fine with it. But I think he's going through something else, and he needs his dad.*

Before Ledger could react, another text rolled in.

Kash: *By the way, I'll let you pass on totally ignoring me when I came through the door since Valon is here. LOL!*

Ledger fought a bright smile as he opened his grocery app. He swore Kash was the biggest miracle worker alive. It was like he had a master's degree in decoding people. Honestly, he probably just knew Valon better than anyone else alive. Still, he had brought Valon home. Ledger couldn't love him more. He placed a rush order. When he looked up, his gaze met Kash's stare, and his soul sang.

"I love you." Kash mouthed the words.

Ledger realized he wore a huge grin. He couldn't believe how happy this one person made him.

Valon made a glass of iced tea before sitting at the island. "It's like you were expecting me. You already had my favorite drink waiting." He took a sip and then spoke over the rim of his glass. "So when are you two getting married, and do I have to call Kash 'Daddy' now?"

A huge guffaw exploded from Kash while Ledger stared at Valon, stunned.

Valon laughed. "You should see your face. That's it. I'm walking into the room every time I see you guys now, saying, *Ooh, Daddy*. You'll never live this down."

Kash still laughed so hard, he was swiping his eyes.

Ledger had no clue how to react. "I'm not frail yet. I can still kick your ass."

Kash somehow laughed even harder. His body shook, but no sound emerged.

Ledger crossed the room and twisted his nipple.

Kash jumped away, rubbing his assaulted chest. "Already abusing me. We aren't even married yet."

So much happiness swam in Kash's eyes that—suddenly—Ledger had never wanted anything more in his life than a lifetime of this. The three of them together, teasing and laughing. This was what a home should look like, and it was because of Kash.

Ledger had to have as much of this as he could get for the rest of his life. "As far as marriage proposals go, that was a pretty piss-poor attempt, but I still accept."

They laughed together.

It was Ledger's turn to swipe his eyes. Yeah. He wanted this forever. Love lived here.

After an awesome meal, they grabbed a bottle of wine and moved to the couch. Valon looked wired but also exhausted, like he hadn't slept in forever, but he still couldn't. Kash picked the recliner so Valon could sit next to his dad.

Valon sat forward with his elbows on his knees, as if he couldn't relax. He pulled a cigarette from the front pocket of his t-shirt. In one glance, Kash knew there was no tobacco inside. He had run that brand for Noir before.

“No smoking in the house.”

At Ledger’s reminder, Valon put it above his ear—like stashing a pencil. He grabbed the notebook Kash had left behind. It sat open where he left off last. “Wow. You’re still doing this?” He flipped through the pages. “While you were pushing me to the top, I should’ve been dragging you with me. I know a few people who would love these. You could do this for a living.”

Ledger didn’t hesitate to jump on the bandwagon. “That would be amazing. He’s talented as hell.”

Kash didn’t know what to say. On one hand, his drawings were private. On the other hand, he was always flattered when anyone thought he could be a professional.

Before he thought of a proper response, Valon stood. "I think I'll head to bed."

Ledger immediately popped to his feet and hugged him. "Goodnight. Try to actually sleep, okay?"

Valon nodded. "I will." He waved in Kash's direction. "Night, Kash."

Kash dipped his chin and mumbled his goodnights. The moment they were alone, Kash stood and took Ledger's hand. "Let's go, sexy. It's bedtime for you too."

Ledger stayed quiet, but he let Kash lead him to the bedroom. Kash had expected Ledger to be bursting with questions.

Instead, he seemed locked in his head. Kash gently shut them inside their room.

Even though it ended up being a fun night, it was also the longest of Kash's life. The moment they were closed off from the world, Kash nearly sighed in relief. He just needed Ledger in his arms.

"You should take off your clothes."

Kash turned at the demand.

Ledger was already nude from the waist up. Kash leaned against the door and looked him up and down, savoring thc show. "Are you trying to seduce me?"

Ledger's eyebrows rose at Kash's question. "No. I'm demanding you to fuck me."

Jesus. He was sexy and a temptation straight from the heavens. "I like this side of you." He straightened away from the door and took off his shirt. Kash tossed it aside. "But I need a shower." Leaving Ledger where he stood, Kash moved to the bedside nightstand and grabbed the lube. He headed for the bathroom without looking back. When he finished undressing, he realized Ledger didn't intend to follow. Kash rolled his eyes.

He stuck his head out the door. Ledger was undressing as if he honestly believed Kash had just turned him down. "Get your ass in here, Ledge. You're moving awfully slow for someone with demands."

Quietly, Ledger moved his way. The way he held Kash's stare every step of the way had Kash breathing harder. His earlier tone should have let him know Ledger wasn't in the mood to play. He didn't want to be cheered up after their stressful day. Ledger wanted to get dicked down. Kash could do that too.

The moment Ledger crossed the threshold into the bathroom, Kash took Ledger's hand and kissed the back of it. He didn't let go as he closed the door and led Ledger to the shower. Kash joked a lot to keep everyone happy, but underneath all of that, Kash preferred quiet and peace. Nothing peaceful was about to happen, especially since shower sex was always over the top with them, but he preferred the seriousness of the moment.

"Get the water going at whatever temperature you like. I'm good with anything."

Ledger silently did as told.

Kash's heart couldn't take it. He molded against Ledger's back. His lips found Ledger's neck. "Damn. It's been hard not to crawl all over you today. I've wanted to kiss this spot for hours."

Ledger reached over his head and held on to the back of Kash's head as if he needed more and couldn't let Kash get away. "I'm about to sound totally insane, okay?"

Kash heard the seriousness in Ledger's tone and treated the conversation as such. "You can tell me anything. I'd never judge you."

"The way I love you makes me wonder if I ever really loved Ry. It's like you showed up at that concert and you woke up all these old feelings I hid in shame. But more than that, every day since, you've brought me peace and happiness like I've never experienced." Ledger took an audible breath. It sounded shaky. "When

I look back on my life, I don't feel this. Only a sad desperation to hold a family together comes with those memories. You've brought me to life, and there's no chance I'll get enough years with you."

The backs of Kash's eyes burned at the genuine ache in Ledger's voice. He corralled Ledger into the shower. "Then I'll find you in the next life." Kash kissed Ledger's nape. "And then the one after that. You're not escaping me." Kash ran his hand down Ledger's torso. When he reached Ledger's cock, he stroked. He licked the shell of Ledger's ear. "I'm sorry no one has loved you properly. But best believe I'm not going anywhere, and I fully intend to make every second of our forever as perfect as possible."

Ledger flattened his palms against the wall and pressed backward, tormenting Kash with his perfect ass.

Kash's hand moved to Ledger's chest, over Ledger's heart. He savored the way it beat against his palm.

"I wish I knew what words to use to vocalize the way I feel." Kash skimmed his lips against Ledger's shoulder. "You've always been the one person who understands me. I never stood a chance against falling in love with you. No one saw me at all until you did. You say no one has loved you like me. I'm pretty certain no one has loved me at all except you." He knew his admission included Valon. That changed nothing. He had said what he meant. Kash grabbed the lube and toyed with Ledger's asshole until he had enough to ease his way. When Ledger's breathing changed, Kash urged Ledger's hips back, bending Ledger to his liking.

They were getting married. Ledger had accepted his proposal, and Kash wouldn't let him take it back.

Kash kissed Ledger's spine as he pressed his way inside. "I'm so goddamn in love with you. It's like I can't see anything else at all. I'm desperate to spend the rest of my life making love to you." Kash thrust. "Holding your hand." He pulled out and thrust again. "Eating across from you." Kash set the pace at Ledger's first moan. "Doing nothing at all with you is a million times better than doing anything at all."

The experience was—oddly—the quietest lovemaking of his life. It was like they were both so focused on every sensation, they couldn't make a sound. They stayed present for every second. Even as Ledger blew and sent Kash to heaven, Kash couldn't do a single thing but try to keep breathing. By the time he came down from the epic high, Ledger already worked at cleaning their bodies. The way he scrubbed Kash's body, getting bubbles and suds going and running down his skin, kept Kash hard. That was a real problem. Now that Kash had Ledger, he couldn't get enough. They kissed as they washed. It was a devouring kiss like they equally couldn't get close enough. Like what they had was so big, there weren't enough outlets.

"I love you." The breathless-sounding proclamation hit the center of Kash's heart. He couldn't hear those words enough.

"I love you too." That claim wasn't strong enough to satiate the possessive beast inside Kash. But those were the only ones he had.

Ledger kissed his neck. "I guess we should get ready for bed."

Kash hugged Ledger to his chest and squeezed. "Yeah. I guess so."

They worked together to turn off the water while the other grabbed towels. With their towels wrapped around their waists, they brushed their teeth side by side.

"I'll grab our pajama pants," Ledger offered as he opened the bathroom door. Their pants were folded and already waiting on the floor right outside the door. There was also a lump in the center of bed. After quickly closing the door, they rushed to get dressed. Neither of them spoke. Kash had no clue how Ledger felt at the moment, but Kash's head was all over the place. Logically, he understood Valon knew about them, but it felt like a whole other thing for Valon to be right outside the door while they had shower sex.

They exchanged glances as if they shared the same thoughts. With nothing left to do, they left the bathroom. Ledger eased into bed next to Valon, obviously trying not to wake him. Kash stood at the edge of the bed trying to decide what to do. Maybe he should sleep somewhere else. This entire thing was a juggling act.

"Can I sleep with you guys?" Valon sounded groggy and barely awake.

Ledger kissed Valon's forehead. "Of course."

Kash eased into bed on Valon's other side. Despite feeling awkward, he was more worried than anything. This was the closest to the old Valon as Kash had seen in years. When they had met back in high school, Valon had been quiet and shy. He was the type who needed protection. While Kash understood Valon had to be a completely different person now to sing in front of thousands of fans and always be in the spotlight, Valon needed a balance between the two. But also, it kind of seemed like Valon still needed protection too. Kash would do what he could.

Valon snuggled closer to Ledger. "I'm sorry."

"For what?" Ledger whispered the question. It was the smart choice since Valon still sounded half asleep.

"For leaving you all those gifts and making you believe you're in more danger than you are. I didn't know how else to get Kash here. He always shows up when people need him."

Ledger stared at Kash over the top of Valon's head. All the silent messages passed between them. Valon had really done this, just as he claimed, and there was something big wrong with him. Something he tried to hide. All they could do was be here, keeping Valon safe while he got the sleep he desperately seemed to need. Kash recognized something real in that moment. These two had always been all he really had. He would die to keep them safe. Whatever it took.

Chapter Thirteen

Kash did his best to slip quietly from the bed, leaving Valon and Ledger behind. The pair needed their sleep, and Kash had some shit to do. After taking a shower in the guestroom, Kash checked on the pair one more time before heading for the living room. He needed to run a quick but important errand before Marc showed up for their meeting. Thankfully, he was out and back home in under half an hour. Marc waited for him in the driveway. Kash climbed out of the SUV and opened the side door for Marc.

Marc was a big, cuddly-looking guy. While he could be a scary motherfucker, he had a sweet edge that Kash knew was needed right now. Marc smiled as he approached. "Hey."

Kash returned the smile. It was genuine. Marc was seriously just a nice guy. "Hey. Odd request, but do you mind joining me in the SUV? I don't want to take any chances of being overheard."

Marc's forehead furrowed, but he didn't argue. "Sure."

Kash waited until they were closed inside the vehicle before jumping right in. "I'd like to hire you to guard Valon." He rushed to clarify. "I mean, you'd still be part of Steel's company. But Steel has agreed to let me steal you and put you with Valon, if you're willing."

"Sure. No problem. What's up?"

Marc needed to know what he walked into, but Kash wasn't sure he came out looking very good in this situation. "Valon is... difficult." Marc nodded, and Kash pressed on. "I also think he has some sort of huge issue going on that he's not talking about. The combination will likely make him a bit of an explosive client."

"No one can be worse than this one bank CEO who made my life absolute hell."

Even though Kash chuckled, he wasn't as sure about that. All of Valon's guards kept quitting for a reason. Considering how well-trained Steel's employees were, Valon had to be something else.

Marc's smile slipped away. "I'm guessing there's a reason we're having this conversation out here. Is Valon against this idea?"

"No, that's not the case at all. He doesn't even know about this plan. I wanted to make sure you're cool with this first. I think the real Valon is still there, hiding behind this spoiled rock star persona. He's nothing like he's been behaving." At least, Kash hoped that was the case. Once upon a time, he thought he knew Valon better than anyone. It was possible the bitterness he witnessed yesterday had changed Valon permanently. Either way... "I think he's one rejection away from being capable of anything. He told me he doesn't have anyone. If you didn't want this job, I couldn't let him hear that."

Marc nodded along. "I get it. He does have the look of someone ready to break." He cleared his throat. "You know the drill. I need to know everything if I'm going to be of any use. It seems like there's been a bit of discourse."

Yeah. This was the part where Kash didn't come out looking the best. Kash cleared his throat. "I met Valon on the first day of his freshman year of high school. He wasn't anywhere near to being where he is now, and I was still starstruck. Valon was scrawny as fuck, but he was adorable. There was just something about him. I wanted to be in his company. He's always been special. You can feel it when you're near him. It's like he was born to be a star. We were a couple until his sophomore year of college."

Marc's eyebrows rose when Kash said "couple," but he didn't speak.

Kash had to get everything out. "A very long story as short as possible, I convinced him to quit college and take a risk on his talent. He did, and a month later, he had a record deal and basically just disappeared. For three months, Ledger and I sat by our phones every day, waiting to hear if he was even alive. He seriously just walked away from us. That's why Ledger keeps his location on his phone now. For real, he just vanished. After three months, I finally broke and hunted him down in L.A. He looked at me like he didn't even know who I was. Valon was too busy for me. He had just 'forgotten' to keep in touch. I knew it was purposeful. He tasted stardom, and I wasn't part of his dream."

"Jesus."

At Marc's quiet curse, Kash took a breath. "Well, I'm marrying his dad now, so..." Kash fought a nervous chuckle. He hated talking about his past. "Valon acts like he's perfectly fine and unbothered. Maybe he is. I don't know him anymore. But I think he's falling apart, and I doubt my marrying his dad is making anything better. I don't know. He just needs a closer eye from someone who can show him grace and keep me in the loop. He's Ledger's son. Ledger's pride and joy. I have to know Valon is safe and in good hands. Ledger is my whole world. I need him to know Valon will be okay."

Marc reached over and squeezed Kash's shoulder. "I'll do what I can."

The door from the kitchen into the garage opened, and Valon peeked out. He looked like an unsure child.

Kash immediately jumped from the vehicle.

Before he could ask a single question, Valon held up a small bag. "Some guy just delivered this for you."

Kash smiled so hard, he almost hopped in place in happiness. "Yes! Come on. I want your opinion on this." Kash steered Valon back inside with Marc on his heels. There was no time like the present to mend what he could while solidifying their family.

Valon looked over his shoulder, obviously confused by Marc's presence.

Kash dropped the news quickly, hoping to move on before Valon could argue. "Valon, Marc. Marc, Valon. I know you two haven't been formally introduced. Marc is your new bodyguard." If Valon could buy Ledger a friend, Kash could buy one for Valon.

Valon flashed Marc a shy-looking smile. "Hi."

"Hey there." Marc sounded calm, peaceful, and friendly.

The way Valon's shoulders relaxed couldn't be missed, making Kash realize how tightly Valon had been holding himself. Relief filled Kash. Everything would be fine. They would make it through this.

The bed shook slightly, startling Ledger awake. His gaze shot to where he had found Valon the night before. Bright sunlight filled the room, and Valon was gone. The shaking had to be from Kash crawling back into bed with him fully dressed, like he had been up for hours. Ledger's gaze slid toward the clock. It was nearly noon. Damn. He never slept late. It seemed all the stress had finally caught up with him.

"Hey. Why are you dressed?"

Kash scooted beneath the blankets and snuggled close. "I had to go out this morning."

Ledger had already decided he wouldn't ask questions anytime Kash had to run out for a quick errand. Ignorance and bliss and all that. He didn't want to know when Kash did anything illegal. Ledger wondered what it said about him that he was so unbothered. Likely nothing good.

"Where's Valon?" He braced himself to hear that Valon had already left. Ledger would never find out what in the hell was going on with him if Valon didn't sit still for a little while.

"He's hanging out in the garage with Marc."

“Marc’s here?” Ledger felt like he had slept for three days and no longer knew his household.

Kash tugged Ledger closer. “Yeah. I talked to him this morning about taking on Valon full time. He’s a talker and is used to snobbish CEOs making his life miserable. I think he’s a good fit with Valon. He’ll treat Valon like a friend while also being unaffected when Valon turns into the raging asshole that’s obviously cost him several bodyguards.”

“Sounds like he’s the perfect choice.”

Kash shifted around as if uncomfortable while answering absently. “I guess we’ll see.” His hand appeared from beneath the covers. “Here.”

It took Ledger a second to focus on the velvet ring box held three inches from his face. “What’s this?”

Kash pulled a confused face. “You accepted my marriage proposal last night. I can’t have you running around here without a ring, letting all these obsessed men think they have a shot.”

Ledger’s mind raced. When had he accepted a marriage proposal? It hit him. They had been joking in the kitchen. Ledger had accepted his proposal. He hadn’t even entertained the idea that Kash was serious. While his thoughts raced, Ledger accepted the box and flipped it open. The last thing he wanted was for Kash to see how scattered his thoughts were. Kash had been neglected and rejected his entire life. Ledger couldn’t add to that by seeming unsure.

It turned out the most beautiful ring Ledger had ever seen waited for him inside. His mind blanked as he pulled out the ring and slipped it onto his finger. It fit perfectly.

Ledger shook his head. “I’m a little scared to ask how you got this gorgeous of a ring in my exact size in one morning.”

Kash’s bright smile proved how important this was to him. “I have connections with connections. All I needed was the ring on your dresser to get a measurement. Do you really like it? It’s not over the top or anything, is it?”

Ledger couldn’t stop staring at the sparkling band on his ring finger. Never in a million years would Ledger have thought to see another marital ring there. Even six months ago, if anyone asked,

Ledger would have said he would rather set himself on fire and run into traffic than be married again. This was completely different, though. It was Kash.

"I love it." The way his voice shook was the nail in the coffin. Ledger had to admit he had never wanted anything as badly as this family they were creating.

Kash kissed his cheek.

A soft knock landed on the bedroom door.

Ledger bit back a sigh. "No rest for the wicked." He turned his head. "Come in!"

The door slowly opened, and Valon stuck his head inside, as if uncertain of his welcome. His hair was in a bun and his face clear of all makeup. As Ledger looked on, one silver curl slipped from the bun and covered his eye. Valon tucked the lock behind his ear.

His gaze was locked on Kash. “Did he love it? We’re dying out here to know.” He stepped fully into the room with Marc on his heels. Valon climbed onto the foot of the bed and sat back on his heels. He focused on Ledger without giving Kash time to answer. “It’s fucking gorgeous, isn’t it? Let me see it on your hand.”

Ledger held out his hand. As he watched Valon look it over with genuine interest, he couldn’t take it anymore. “You’re really okay with this, aren’t you?”

Valon’s forehead furrowed as he met Ledger’s stare. “Of course. I set this up.”

Ledger shook his head. “I don’t understand why you seem so unbothered.”

Valon shifted positions and sat cross-legged. He looked stone-cold serious about the topic. His gaze moved to Kash. "It really was a lifetime ago, huh?"

"Yeah." Kash sounded slightly sad, like a nod to a past that mattered but could never exist again.

Valon looked Ledger's way. "It feels like fifty years have passed in the last few years. So many good, bad, and unbelievable things have happened." His gaze seemed to turn inward. "Sometimes I don't know which of those things I've had the most of, but I know one thing." His expression shifted again, as if coming back to the present. "It turns out you two are the only people who have ever loved me for real. One night, I stared at the ceiling, unable to sleep. You can close your ears for half a second on this one, if you'd like, Dad." Unfortunately, he didn't actually pause to give Ledger time to cover his ears. "Admittedly, I was high as a kite to the point I didn't think I'd ever come down. It was one of those crazy things where I was so out of it, I felt like I floated on a different plane and saw my life with zero emotion attached. Do you know what I saw?"

Again, he didn't have any time to answer. "I saw you two sacrificing everything for me, even when I definitely didn't deserve it. Most especially when I didn't deserve it. I saw you two sit quietly by, encouraging me, while I built a life that would barely include you, if at all. Meanwhile, all you two really had was each other and all the pain I caused."

Valon focused on Kash. "You're right. Silence is its own form of violence. In the silence that night, I realized how truly fucked up I am."

"Baby, that's not true." Ledger couldn't hear Valon say anything bad about himself. It hurt his heart too badly.

A sad smile passed over Valon's lips.

Marc leaned against the doorframe with an expression that screamed he didn't judge.

Kash stared at Valon as if studying for a test.

Ledger couldn't stop taking in every detail.

Valon took his hand. The moment had the whole I'm-going-to-hold-your-hand-while-I-say-this vibe. "I need you to be happy. Please do this one thing for me and have the life you deserve. Let this be one time I didn't—" Valon stopped and took a second. "I need to know you're happy." His gaze moved Kash's way. "I need to know we're still friends."

"There's never been a day you couldn't call me." Kash sounded gruff, as if trying but failing to hide his emotions.

Valon brightened. "You two should enjoy your day." He jumped out of bed. "I'm going to show Marc the studio here where I recorded my first album. When I called earlier, they said I could use whatever they have available if I just need some inspiration to write something new. It could be fun to get back to the basics."

Ledger nodded along, wondering when his son had developed a split personality.

"Have a good time. I'll see you when you get back."

With a smile and a wave, Valon was out the door.

Ledger and Kash looked each other's way. For a moment, they simply held each other's stare. Then, simultaneously, they settled in to snuggle. Tucked beneath Kash's arm, Ledger trailed his fingertip up and down Kash's torso, drawing invisible pictures.

"Welp." Kash's sexy voice broke the silence. "This has been a very enlightening yet confusing visit."

Ledger took a steadying breath. He had to believe everything would be okay. "At least I know my son is still in there. I think he'll talk to us when he's ready. You know Valon can't sit still."

"Or stay quiet when he's comfortable with people," Kash said with a deep chuckle that vibrated against the ear Ledger had pressed to his chest.

A genuine smile popped to Ledger's lips. "Yeah." He made it two heartbeats. "When are we getting married? I know you. You have a plan."

"This one time, I think I'll let you help make some decisions."

Ledger couldn't stop smiling due to the happiness in Kash's voice alone. "You've never had a wedding, so..."

"Who the fuck would I invite to a wedding?" Kash sounded genuinely confused.

"Thank God. I never want to go through the stress of matching flowers with napkins and bow ties ever again. That shit sucks the life right out of you." After his rant, guilt set in. He shouldn't talk about his past, and Kash deserved a huge wedding. He would only have the one. "But I'd be proud as hell to have you at my side in front of a huge venue that someone else put together."

Kash didn't respond right away. When he did, he sounded kind of dreamy rather than any reaction Ledger had been panicking over. "Do you remember the night before I broke down and drove to L.A. to confront Valon?"

Ledger couldn't forget that night. They had almost kissed, or at least it had felt that way to Ledger. He had thought about that night way more than was probably healthy, trapped between longing and knowing that was the moment that had broken Kash. That almost-kiss was the catalyst that changed the course of their lives.

"Yeah. We went to the bookstore and got ice cream afterward."

"I mean after that," Kash said, pushing Ledger to focus on the moment that could have gone so many ways.

"We went to the beach, sat in the sand, and listened to the crashing waves." Ledger swore he still felt every emotion from that night. Every sound still lived in his ears.

"I was enraged at the unfairness of life." Ledger froze at Kash's confession. Kash kept talking, changing Ledger's view of what happened. "You were always so sad, and I was hurt and fucking furious." His tone backed up his claim. "Frustration boiled hotter and bigger inside me with every second that passed. All because I realized how hopeless everything was. I'd spent years thinking I built some kind of future with Valon, only to find out too late that I spent more time building a life with you than him, and it was a life I would never have." His muscles relaxed. His tone softened. "But then I looked at you and you looked at me, and I thought, one day, I'll marry him. I had no idea how long it would take, but I knew you were the one. Back then, that was probably the most heartbreaking moment of my life. Now, I think maybe that's where we should get married."

Ledger's whole chest warmed. He hadn't even suspected that was where Kash's confessions were headed. But Kash was right, and Ledger could already picture it.

"Just us with Valon as our witness. That sounds beautiful."

Kash somehow managed to snuggle even closer. "Yeah. It'll be perfect. You'll see."

Ledger closed his eyes and drew Kash's life force into his lungs. He felt more at peace than he could vocalize.

"Do you think Valon looked too skinny?"

Kash's entire body shook with laughter at Ledger's question. "You couldn't handle it, could you? Five minutes of peace max, and then you have to worry about something."

Ledger huffed.

Kash rolled, pinning Ledger beneath him. He slid down the bed and blew raspberries on Ledger's stomach. Ledger laughed and twisted, fighting for his life to get away. By the time Kash stopped tormenting Ledger, Ledger was on his stomach, crushed beneath Kash's weight. His playful tickling turned into sweet kisses. Ledger smiled so hard, his face hurt. If Ledger knew nothing else, he knew he didn't deserve this massive happiness, who weighed too much to be acting like Ledger's blanket. God, he fucking wanted it, though. Ledger would do whatever it took to keep this.

It never took long for loving kisses to turn heated between them. The air practically crackled with need. Kash's body was on fire. He sat back on his knees and peeled off his shirt before he went back to nibbling on Ledger's back.

"I'm an old man." The words sounded like Ledger faked crying.

Kash chuckled against Ledger's back at the statement. "Shut up."

Ledger laughed. "I was about to say, I'm an old man, but I swear my libido has never been higher. Fuck, you keep me hard."

"Good. The feeling is mutual. I shouldn't have to suffer alone." Kash moved lower, kissing every bump of Ledger's spine. He peeled off Ledger's pajama pants in the process.

When he sank his teeth into Ledger's ass cheek, Ledger moaned. "Damn, Kash. You know I love it."

Kash knew everything Ledger liked. He would not disappoint. Once he had Ledger's pants off, Kash stood and peeled off his jeans. He moved to lock the door too. No one believed in privacy around here. With Ledger splayed on his stomach, waiting for Kash, Kash somehow got harder at the sight. He grabbed the lube and settled between Ledger's legs. Kash urged Ledger onto his knees. The moment he had the asshole that belonged to him on display, Kash didn't hold back. He dove in face first. The sound Ledger made had Kash's dick leaking. Kash swore he walked away from every sexual encounter with Ledger never remembering anything except how much Ledger made him feel.

"Goddamn, Kash. That feels good. You're fucking amazing with that tongue."

Kash pulled away and brought the lube into play. "I'm amazing with every part of my body. You shouldn't forget it." He fingered Ledger's asshole.

Another deep moan muffled by pillow caressed Kash's ears. "As if anyone could forget this."

The way Ledger always stroked his ego was a massive high. A thought hit, almost ruining the moment. "You're probably still sore. I shouldn't do this."

Ledger's head shot up. He glared at Kash over his shoulder. "Are you fucking kidding me? Get inside of me, right now."

A smile exploded across Kash's face. "Yes, sir. The boss has spoken." Kash got to work pressing his way inside before Ledger had time to argue. He didn't like being called the boss, but he was. Ledger ruled every second of Kash's life. As he went hilt deep, the memory of the way Ledger had looked at him while sitting on the beach overwhelmed him again. That was the first time Kash had seen Ledger look at him with the same longing Kash secretly carried. He kissed Ledger's back again and waited for the urge to cry to pass. Kash slowly rocked inside Ledger, doing his best to make sure he hit that hotspot inside.

Ledger whimpered.

The lump in Kash's throat grew bigger. He could never tell anyone how much he had felt that night. It was like the sound of the ocean blocked out the world. Kash had stared at Ledger, and love alongside the unfairness of it all had cut through Kash. He had seen his future with Ledger and hadn't known how to get here. Now he was set to marry Ledger, and he couldn't believe it. No one could know how he had ached. That night, reality had landed on Kash like an anvil, crushing him as he realized—for the first time in his life—someone genuinely loved him, and he couldn't have him.

Before Kash saw it coming, he found himself on his back with Ledger staring down at him, looking worried. "Why are you crying?"

Kash hadn't even noticed. He sniffed. "You're marrying me. You're really doing it."

Ledger's expression cleared. He lowered himself onto Kash's erection, making every muscle in Kash's abdomen flex with lust. Ledger's gaze never moved from holding Kash's stare. "I'm really marrying you. It can't happen fast enough. Since our wedding isn't today, the best I can do is make love to you while hoping you feel how much you're cherished."

Ledger made it hard to think, much less overthink. The way he rode Kash had him aroused beyond using his brain.

Ledger's expression turned into the hottest of porn. His cheeks were flushed, and his lips slightly parted. He tilted his chin up—like there wasn't enough oxygen to support how close he was. Kash could watch him all day.

"That's it, beautiful. Ride me. I want to wear your cum. Fuck, you're beautiful when you blow. Let me see it."

The cords of Ledger's neck strained. He was so close, Kash swore he could taste Ledger's orgasm. When it hit, Kash gasped. The way Ledger's asshole felt as he spit cum was like seeing heaven.

When Kash exploded, he couldn't look away from Ledger as he pumped him full of cum. Ledger was his forever. Kash wanted to shout it to the world.

The expression Valon wore while strumming a guitar was mesmerizing. Marc was man enough to admit he was starstruck. Valon's curly silver hair was in a bun, but the shorter curls in the front kept escaping. Valon looked lost and sad. Young and vulnerable. Damn. He was only five years younger than Marc. Why did he look so young? Valon just seemed so fresh-faced and innocent. The person in front of him didn't match the man Marc had watched on stage. He didn't know if he should say he had been to a few of Valon's concerts and ruin the moment. Maybe the mask would fall back into place if he knew Marc was a fan. He liked this version too much to watch Valon hide.

"What do you enjoy doing?" Valon's chin lifted. His dark blue eyes latched onto Marc as if he had never disappeared inside his music.

Marc had to search his mind with Valon looking at him as if he really cared. "Um. I like football. Watching, not playing."

Valon smiled, making the world seem brighter. “Really? You look like you’ve played a game or two in your life.”

“I have. That was back in high school, though.”

“What made you stop at high school level?”

Marc shrugged. “Reality hit. Not everyone has what it takes to make it to pro level. I didn’t have what it takes.”

Valon’s gaze moved over Marc’s face. “I wonder where I’d be right now if Kash hadn’t forced me past that belief.” He strummed the guitar absentmindedly while staring into space. It was like he went somewhere else for a moment before his gaze returned to Marc. “Don’t mind me. I always overthink everything. You seem like a nice person. You deserved to have your dreams come true. I didn't." He looked down at his hands, as if he couldn't handle anyone looking at him any longer.

Marc felt the loss of his attention. He wanted Valon's eyes on him. "Is it okay if I ask you a personal question?"

When Valon's chin lifted this time, he was smiling again. "You're about to be very personally in my life all hours of the day, so I'd say it's fine."

He supposed that was true. Keeping someone as hugely popular as Valon safe would take a lot more than he had ever given. "You can always tell me to mind my business. I won't be offended. Are you unhappy where you are?"

Valon's smile turned fake.

Marc immediately regretted the question, most especially when Valon answered.

"Why would I be unhappy? I'm a star."

Valon shrugged. "So? Both can be true at the same time. You're still a person with feelings, like everyone else."

For a moment, Valon went back to watching his fingers on the guitar strings. Finally, he looked up again. "How do you see being with me all the time going?"

The question wasn't sarcastic, or sound like he was about to remind Marc he was the boss. So, Marc treated it as genuine. "Well, you're the boss. It's my job to keep you safe, and I expect at least some cooperation in that. I don't want you to get hurt, but if you don't want me to watch you, I won't see a thing. I'm not here to micromanage you or judge you. In fact, I *won't* judge you or think badly of you for doing whatever, as long as you're not hurting anyone else. Just be you. Pretend I'm not here when it suits you. But if you want to be friends, I'd like that too."

Marc swore he saw a weight lift from Valon's shoulders. Valon never looked away from him. "No. I'm not happy."

Marc dipped his chin and acknowledged the words. "Okay. We'll work on that."

A sweet smile touched Valon's lips. He went back to his music. After a moment, he began to sing while Marc stared at him in awe. He saw what Ledger and Kash meant. Valon had something that made him special. In his presence, it was undeniable. But something about this life was killing him. Marc wouldn't stop until he found out what.

Chapter Fourteen

As much as Kash loved hanging out in bed with Ledger, they couldn't be lazy forever. They had to face the day. While Ledger showered, Kash worked on his latest sketch. For some reason, he couldn't get the shading quite right. It was like the colors were creating opposing emotions than he tried to portray.

A barely audible shuffle or dragging noise had Kash's head shooting up. It took a second for him to puzzle through whether he was hearing things or not. Yeah. He had definitely heard something. It had sounded like a package being delivered. Kash waited a moment longer, expecting the doorbell to ring. When it didn't, he set the sketchbook aside and moved to check the peephole. He didn't see anyone. Kash pulled open the door just to be safe. A vase of red roses waited next to an open box full of various cooking supplies. Kash stared at the gifts, confused as fuck.

Ledger appeared over his shoulder. He peeked around Kash's side. "What the fuck? Surely Valon didn't send anything else."

They shared a look.

Ledger pulled out his phone and tapped on the face. After a moment, he shook his head. "Valon swears it wasn't him."

They held each other's gaze before simultaneously looking toward the items on the porch.

Ledger found his words first. "What do we do?"

Kash appreciated Ledger deferring to him. No matter what else went on in their lives, Kash was still Ledger's bodyguard. His security for life. "Let me look over everything to make sure it's safe. If I don't find anything shady, it's up to you what we do. I can trash it all if that's what you choose."

Ledger nodded. "Yeah, okay." He still looked unnerved. That got under Kash's skin.

"Do we have any latex gloves or even those rubber gloves for cleaning? There's a chance someone is watching us right now. Their plan might've been to drug you and then drag you into the house. I won't risk anything being tainted with fentanyl."

Kash wished he hadn't explained himself quite so much when Ledger went pale. "Um, yeah. I think the first-aid kit has latex gloves."

Kash tried taking Ledger's fear down a notch. "Great thinking, sexy. Grab those. I've got this. You're not in any danger."

Ledger nodded, but he still looked upset when he walked away. Thankfully, he was back in a flash.

"Thanks, angel." He kept his tone light as he reached for the gloves, as if there wasn't anything wrong. Kash pulled on the gloves and started sifting. Everything appeared brand new. Each item still had a price tag and was a high-dollar purchase. "This is definitely odd as fuck. My guess is this came from a fan who wants to support your work. I doubt anyone who means you harm would buy you something so expensive and perfect for you."

Kash lifted the box. A card was underneath. "For fuck's sake. I should've looked for that first." Kash opened the envelope. "This mother-" Kash rolled his eyes and stuffed the card underneath his arm. He pulled off his gloves as he stood. "It's from Ry."

Ledger stepped out and stood close enough for them to read the note together.

Hey, babydoll,

I spent some time thinking about our fight and your relationship with Kash. Obviously, I know what you see in him. I tried hard to get him into bed too. It's always been difficult for me to resist a pretty face. You're owed this one affair. Now we've spent some years playing, and it's time to let me come home. I bought you these gifts to show how much I support your new career. You always had my back with the gym. Let me have yours now. Please, just think about it. We've been apart long enough.

I'll always love you.

Ry

They looked each other's way at the same time, wearing matching looks of annoyance and disgust. Ledger broke first.

"My affair. As if we never got divorced and just letting things cool down. For years, apparently."

Kash shook his head. He didn't even know what to say. Ry's bullshit was easily the most ridiculous crap he had ever seen. That was saying a lot since he had collected money from people who had nothing left thanks to drugs.

Unexpectedly, Ledger started laughing. Kash looked his way with raised eyebrows. Ledger laughed harder. He tried to speak and failed. Kash couldn't help but smile at the show. Ledger's laughter was genuine.

"Do you plan to let me in on the joke?"

Ledger held one finger up while he tried to get himself under control. "This dumb motherfucker really thinks I'd choose him. He really believes I've spent every day since our divorce waiting for him to get done playing. How fucking pathetic." He swiped his eyes. His laughter faded as he met and held Kash's gaze. "I really love you. More than I can say. Even though this entire mess with Ry is almost comical, his desperation makes me realize I've never been happier in my life." His hands rose and fell. He looked at a loss for words. "I spent my life waiting for you. I just didn't know it. You're the one who's my other half. I've just been waiting for you to come back to me."

Kash tossed the card in the box and closed the space between them. He poured his entire heart and soul into the kiss he claimed. Ledger really was Kash's everything. He was the only peace and shelter Kash had ever found against a cruel world. Ledger truly had been right here in Kash's hometown, waiting for when they would be a they. It was a real shame he hadn't killed Ry years ago. But he supposed this moment never would've happened if he had.

Kash's lips moved to Ledger's cheek. He couldn't move even a step away. All he wanted was to stay right here forever.

"That's the plan."

A smile exploded across Kash's lips. "I didn't mean to say that out loud. You really scramble my brain. It doesn't even know what my mouth is doing anymore."

Ledger chuckled. "I feel like I'm missing a golden opportunity here to say, 'I'll show what that mouth can do.' But I'm not that type of guy."

Kash threw his head back and roared with laughter at Ledger's fuckboy impression. "Oh, my God. We'll have the best life."

Ledger's eyes swam with laughter. Kash was so fucking in love with him. Every day, he couldn't wait to see what happened next. He would be here for every second of their beautiful future. Ledger would never get rid of him now.

"Let's do something fun."

"Oh, I'm in." Kash was so fucking in. He didn't give a fuck what they did as long as they were together.

Sitting hip to hip, Ledger waved at his phone clipped to the ring light. He knew the smile he wore was huge as hell. Ledger was happy, and he wanted the world to know it. He needed them to know why.

"Hey, everyone. I had to cut our live short yesterday. My baby deserves a proper introduction, and he doesn't like the spotlight." Ledger looked Kash's way to check his reaction. He nearly made Ledger forget his plans. They were shirtless and playing to Ledger's thirst-trap audience. Ledger realized this would mean people would likely stalk the fuck out of him now, but he couldn't brush off what happened yesterday. Kash meant way too much to Ledger.

He forced his gaze back to the camera. "On that note, I'd love for you all to meet my soon-to-be husband, Kash." He looked over, handing the floor to Kash.

Kash's mouth lifted at one corner. Ledger stared at the smoking-hot man Kash had become. "Hey. Maybe stop sending my man disgusting DMs. He's not free to play."

A nervous chuckle escaped Ledger. He hadn't expected that one, but he should have. That's who Kash was. Man, he hoped no one noticed the way Ledger's nipples hardened. He adored that possessive growl in Kash's tone.

"You heard it here first."

A sexy laugh rumbled over him. Fuck. He should have known the moment he had Kash remove a single article of clothing, Ledger would turn into a desperate mess ready to climb him like a tattooed tree.

Ledger cleared his throat. He tried to get back on track. "This is him. Kash doesn't have any social media. He doesn't like it. But he's a bit of a badass, so I wouldn't consider stalking him anyhow." He was serious. Kash wouldn't put up with anyone trying to come between them. That absolute truth landed on him like a ton of bricks. He had to wrap this up. Ledger saw all the hearts flying across the screen.

He knew this would be a hit if he stayed, but being punched in the chest by reality had him feeling needy. "That's all I had for today. I just wanted you guys to meet Kash. That way, if he accidentally gets caught on a live again, you'll know who he is. I'll be back in a few days with a new recipe. Until then, love you guys and be safe." He ended the feed.

For a moment, Ledger stared at nothing, letting his new life sink in. For twenty years, off and on, Ledger had lived in silent torture, wondering if Ry cheated and why. That really wasn't his life anymore. He didn't even realize his entire thinking about relationships had changed overnight until now. Ledger trusted Kash like no one else. Kash wasn't playing. He would never cheat. That wasn't him. He was rock steady and all the way in this future marriage. Ledger really had this amazing life. He passed the threshold of feeling like this couldn't be real to this was absolutely his life now. Ledger would never get enough.

"Are you okay?"

Ledger pulled away from his thoughts and focused on Kash. Kash looked worried. Ledger couldn't have that. "I'm perfect. In fact, life has never been this wonderful. Let's go back to the boardwalk. I think I want some cotton candy." He felt so fucking young.

A bright smile exploded across Kash's face. "If my prince wants cotton candy, that's what he'll get." As Kash pulled his shirt back on, Ledger couldn't look away. Love swelled in his chest. This was until death do they part. Ledger wanted to live forever.

Keep an eye out for the next Steel Security, *His One and Only*

About the Author

Charity Parkerson is an award-winning and multi-published author with several companies. Born with no filter from her brain to her mouth, she decided to take this odd quirk and insert it in her characters. One of her greatest loves is writing morally gray characters. You'll find them scattered throughout her hundreds of titles.

*Nine-time Readers' Favorite Award Winner

*2015 Passionate Plume Award Finalist

*2013 Reviewers' Choice Award Winner

*2012 ARRA Finalist for Favorite Paranormal Romance

*Five-time winner of The Mistress of the Darkpath

Connect with her online:

*Sign up for her newsletter: https://bit.ly/charityparkersonnewsletter

*Join her readers' group on Facebook: http://bit.ly/CharitysTribe

*Website: https://www.charityparkerson.com

*A list of her social media accounts and giveaways all in one place: http://hy.page/charityparkerson

www.ingramcontent.com/pod-product-compliance
Lightning Source LLC
LaVergne TN
LVHW010637110826
845149LV00014B/2858

* 9 7 8 1 9 5 9 5 7 6 8 2 2 *